TO CLAIM THE LONG-LOST LOVER

THE DIAMOND AND THE DOCTOR

JUDE KNIGHT

ISBN: 978-0-9951453-9-9

Created with Vellum

To Sue, the sister of my blood, my dearest friend, and to all the sisters of my heart.

For there is no friend like a sister
In calm or stormy weather;
To cheer one on the tedious way,
To fetch one if one goes astray,
To lift one if one totters down,
To strengthen whilst one stands.

Christina Rosetti, Goblin Market, 1862

TO CLAIM THE LONG-LOST LOVER

The beauty known as the Winderfield Diamond hides a ruinous secret. Society's newest viscount holds the key.

Sarah Winderfield has refused every suitor since Nathaniel Beauclair convinced her to run away with him seven years ago, and then disappeared without a word or a trace. But now she needs a husband. She has a child to love and to protect, and the child needs a father.

She does not expect to meet Nate also on the marriage mart. Should she let him explain? Can she believe him?

Dragged back to England to feed his father's pride in family, Nate refuses to give into the man's demands that he take a wife. Those who beat and abducted him seven years ago said the only woman he will ever love would be married within the month to a husband chosen by her father.

But when he finds that Sarah is still single, he rushes to London. Surely, they can find again the promise they believed in when they were young?

Through a labyrinth of old rumours and new enemies, two long-lost lovers must decide whether or not to claim one another, and win the bright future they both desire.

PREFACE

April 1814

Sarah sat in the secretaries' room, waiting for His Grace's visitors to leave. "I shall tell the duke you want a moment of his time, my lady," offered the man in charge, one of the Duke of Winshire's foreign retainers. Sarah told him not to interrupt the meeting. The last thing she needed was to begin a painful interview with His Grace annoyed at her.

Uncle James is not like father and grandfather, she told herself. If she didn't believe that, she wouldn't be here, kicking her heels while each minute took an hour to creep by. Still, her heart pounded and her hands perspired. A lifetime of experience assured her that men were erratic, and powerful men expected her to sacrifice her own needs and wishes to their whims.

Not Uncle James, Charlotte had insisted. *In any case, you have no choice. If you want money to start a new life, he will need to give his permission. He certainly isn't going to do so without knowing your reasons.* Charlotte had always been the braver twin, despite outward appearances.

She had offered to see the duke with Sarah. Up in the little sitting room of the chambers they shared, Sarah had refused. If she took Charlotte with her as support, how could she convince Uncle

James she was capable of striking out on her own? Now, growing more anxious by the minute, Sarah wished for her sister's supportive presence.

The murmur of voices in the other room grew louder. Sarah leapt to her feet as the duke's door opened. A group of gentlemen exited, almost walking backwards as they assured His Grace of their goodwill, their co-operation, their thanks for his condescension in meeting them himself rather than sending an agent.

For a brief moment, Sarah wondered what they were talking about, but then the duke smiled at her from his doorway, and her own business with him consumed her again.

One of the secretaries took over to usher the guests out, and the Duke of Winshire held out his hand to Sarah. "You wished to see me, Lady Sarah? Come in, and I shall send for tea."

Sarah firmly tamped down the urge to flee. She entered the duke's study, breathing a little more steadily once she was inside. The room bore little resemblance to the lair to which she had been summoned by her grandfather when he decided to personally communicate his expectations, or to rebuke her for failing them.

It had been redecorated to the taste of its new incumbent. The great desk from behind which the former duke had handed down his edicts had been replaced. Light streamed in windows previously obscured day and night by heavy curtains.

His Grace underscored how much he differed from his father by not directing Sarah to the supplicant position before the desk and ensconcing himself behind it. Instead, he led her to a comfortable chair by the fire and took the one opposite.

The changes in decor weren't enough to keep the memories at bay. Sarah could feel what little confidence she had leaking away, taking coherent thought with it. She must have shut her eyes, because her lids flew open when the duke leapt to his feet, saying, "This won't do." He was already out of his chair and striding for the door to the anteroom.

"Zagreb, I am taking my niece to the blue parlour. Redirect our afternoon tea, please. If I am late for the appointment with Mr

Chalmers, please make my apologies. Ask him if he would like to visit the stallion he enquired about while he waits."

Sarah blinked at him as he returned to stand before her, holding out his hand. His nod and his gentle smile reassured her. She allowed him to help her to her feet, place her hand on his sleeve and conduct her to the private door on the inner wall of the room—the one that led to the servant's corridors.

"This was a room of horrors, Sarah, was it not?" He smiled down at her. "My father mostly ignored his children, and I must suppose his grandchildren, too. But when he did notice us, it was never to praise. Only to berate and punish." He lifted a brow in question, and Sarah nodded, his understanding soothing her as much as leaving the office behind them.

He let them into the blue parlour, one of the smaller reception rooms on this business floor of the mansion that was their London home.

Sarah had recovered enough for an apology. "I am sorry to take you from your work, Your Grace. Uncle James, I mean."

The duke shrugged. "The work exists to provide for those who are part of the duchy, Sarah. From you and the rest of my family to the least tenant's child and the youngest scullery maid. If I cannot make time for the people, and particularly for my own family, there is no point to the work."

Her grandfather, father, and brother had assumed the duchy and all its dependents existed to provide for them: for their wealth, power and pleasure. Mulling on that, and its costs to her and all she held dear, she barely noticed the aide delivering the tray. She started when her uncle handed her a cup of tea he had prepared himself.

The gesture—a man of his stature doing women's work—reassured her as nothing else had. She blurted her errand. "Uncle James, I want my dowry. I want to retire to the country so I can raise my son myself."

The duke's only reaction was a slight widening of the eyes. He took a sip of his own tea before he responded. "Your son. Are you with child, Sarah? Or has a great nephew been hidden from me these past two years since I arrived in England?"

The phrasing of the last question broke the dam on Sarah's resentment and it burst out. "He has been hidden from *me* these past six years, sir. Since the day he was born and taken from me, though I begged to hold him just one time." She stopped to blink back angry tears.

His Grace reached for her hand, and held it gently. "Tell me." His voice was warm and concerned, and she found the words came easily at last.

"My grandfather ordered him put out to foster. Mama assured me that she had met the couple herself, but then the duke gave them money to move away, and she could not find out where they went. When you reinstated my pin money after the duke died, I hired an enquiry agent to find him. I just wanted to know that he was well and cared for."

She swallowed, remembering the skinny, frightened, angry little waif that the agent, Mrs Wakefield, had introduced her to that morning. Searching her uncle's eyes for condemnation and scorn, she saw nothing but compassion. "I take it he was not," he commented.

"The foster parents my mother approved died last year. Their relatives did not want Elias—that's what his foster parents called him—so he had been put into the parish orphan asylum. Mrs Wakefield said it was a dreadful place, and she could not leave him there." Sarah clutched at her uncle's arm. "I want to keep him, Uncle James. I can go somewhere I am not known, change my name, pretend to be a widow…"

The duke smiled. "We can do better than that, my dear. Did I not just say that the duchy is here to serve the family? And your little Elias is family."

1

—————

October 1814

"You must at least go up to London and look over the current crop," Nate's father said, for perhaps the third time during this interminable dinner alone.

His father had been delivering instructions and advice since Nate took up residence at Three Oaks, the estate of the Earls of Lechton. Nate had found that the technique he developed during the early years of his enforced naval service worked just as well on the pompous fool who had sired him. He made pleasant noises, while failing to offer any commitment, and listened just enough to ensure he didn't trip over his own cleverness.

Most people, and his father was certainly among their number, were so convinced of their own superiority that it never occurred to them a subordinate might be quietly disagreeing with everything they said. They required only that said subordinate smiled agreeably and gave a vague nod from time to time.

"You need a wife, Bentham. Three sons, m' brothers had between them and all of them single." Nod. Nate could agree that his cousins had been single.

"You need to marry some well-behaved girl with wide hips," Nate's father insisted, "and bed her till you get a son on her."

It didn't work for you, Nate refrained from saying. His father had inherited the earldom thanks to the marital dereliction and deaths of his three nephews. He was determined that the Lechton line would continue through what he insisted on calling 'the fruit of my loins'. The well-behaved girl he'd taken to wife once he inherited had produced three sickly daughters at twelve-month intervals, birthing the third with such difficulty she was unlikely to ever get with child again.

That left Nate, the banished son of his first marriage. Perhaps, as Lord Lechton claimed, he really did believe that Nate had died at sea. "I had only the frailest of hopes when I contacted the navy, my dear Bentham," he had explained. "Imagine my delight to discover you were not only alive, but in Edinburgh."

He had set the hospital where Nate worked into turmoil by writing to reclaim him under Nate's honorary title as heir. To be fair, being called Bentham was better than 'fruit of my loins', as if Nate existed only by reference to his father.

Mind you, that was certainly Lord Lechton's view. His world had revolved around himself when he was merely the Reverend Miles Beauclair, third son of an earl and vicar of three little villages on the ducal estate of one of the earl's friends. His world view had not expanded when he came into his unexpected inheritance.

Nate smiled agreeably, masking his thoughts. *You doomed your own hopes when you betrayed me seven years ago*. And then the earl dropped a name Nate had never expected to hear again.

"I hope you're not thinking about taking up with Sarah Winderfield again. It just won't do. No. I cannot like the connection for you. She's too old now, and a bloody reformer. Anyway, her uncle, the new duke, is not precisely the thing. A seventeen-year-old fresh on the market. That's what you want. We'll be able to train her up the way she should go." He grimaced. "It will be a nuisance to have an unschooled female around the house again, but I suppose I can always go up to London."

Nate sat stunned speechless, his mind blank of everything except the sound of Sarah's name, echoing inside his head. His father kept talking, totally unaware that Nate had stopped listening.

'Sarah Winderfield', his father had said. Nate had been so certain she had long since been married off to someone else. Married, and out of his reach, with—no doubt—a parcel of children in her nursery, and a doting husband. Of course, her husband would be doting. Even a man chosen by that unthinkably arrogant sod, Sutton, and the cruel monster who sired him could not help but dote on a woman as lovely in her nature as she was in appearance.

Sarah Winderfield. All these years he'd been striving to forget her and she had never married? It had been almost the last thing he heard as her father's thugs kicked him into unconsciousness under the supervision of her brother. "My sister is not for the likes of you. Forget her. She will be married within a month to a man of her station."

He had wondered who it was. The sailors he served with were not the sort to collect London Society gossip, and even once he returned to the British Isles, to Edinburgh, he'd made no effort to find out. All that made life bearable was imagining Sarah was happy and well, even if some other man was giving her that happiness in his place.

He would stay out of Society, he had decided—avoid any place where he might see her. His continued existence put her well-being and that of her family at risk, and he wouldn't see her hurt for the world.

And all the time, she had remained unwed. *They did not marry her to someone else.* His mind caught up with another useful pearl mixed in with the pig swill his father had been spouting—*Her father must be dead.* 'Her uncle, the new Duke.' And not just her father, Lord Sutton, but his father, the Duke of Winshire. *They must both be dead.* And her brother, thrice-damned Elfingham, whose riding crop had slashed his face that dreadful day, leaving a cut that became infected so he still bore the scar.

His father had asked a question. The sound of his voice was fresh enough in Nate's memory that he could replay it. "So, when will you leave? What's keeping you here? Not your stupid 'medical clinic', I hope. An earl's heir playing at doctor."

Nate ignored the usual slur on his profession, and on the clinic he had set up in the local village. *Leave for where?* "I beg your pardon?"

"Are you listening to me, boy? I'm telling you, best go now. Parliament has been called for the eighth of November, and if you're at the starting gates you'll have a chance to look the fillies over before anyone else can scoop them up."

Would Sarah Winderfield be in London? Even if not, London was the best place to find out where she was. "You'll be going up for Parliament, my lord?" *And what kind of an ass thought being addressed as 'my lord' by his only son was a compliment?*

Lord Lechton waved a pudgy hand. "I think not. Bad weather for travelling. No, I'll go up in the Spring. Not much to the House, now the war is over."

Over in Europe, at least. There was still fighting in America. And from what Nate had seen as he had travelled here from Scotland, the next job facing Parliament would be winning the peace. *The number of crippled men in tattered uniforms begging on the streets is a scandal and a crime.* They weren't the only signs that the poor had paid the costs of repeated wars with France over the past thirty years. *Come to that, London might be an even better place to practice medicine than here in Lechford.*

"When will you leave?" his father repeated.

Even without his new quest to find Sarah, the opportunity to escape his father's company was too good to miss. "Tomorrow morning, my lord," Nate said.

The Winderfield twins had shared a sitting room since they first moved from the school room floor. From the day of their debut, it had been a retreat in the long and silent battle with their father and grandfather to resist an unwanted marriage.

Now they were free to pursue their own concerns, their work

frequently separated them. Sarah laboured to further the cause of women whose natural protectors were absent or predatory. Charlotte gave the same dedication to bringing education to those denied it by their sex or their place in society.

Their private room became a place where they could relax with the one person in the whole world who would always love and never judge. Even after Sarah moved earlier this year to a lodge in the grounds of one of the duchy's smaller estates, she still had a place in her uncle's homes, and the private sitting room was still a retreat.

Her visits to London had become rare but busy, as she travelled to meetings and entertainments in search of donors and political supporters, and Charlotte went to different events and also inspected establishments she supported, where she often rolled her sleeves up to be of practical assistance.

Here, in their sanctuary, they could share their day, and enjoy the insights of the other, laughing over trials that seemed far more tolerable when shared with a dearest friend.

Today, Sarah was silent as Charlotte made an entertaining story out of a visit to a school on the edges of the slums of St Giles. Sarah's mind wasn't on it. She needed to tell Charlotte what she decided, and for once, she could not predict her sister's reaction.

Charlotte noticed, of course. She trailed off, her changeable hazel eyes—so much more interesting than Sarah's pale blue— sparkling gold in the candlelight as she put her head to one side. "You have something on your mind, Sarah. What is it?"

Sarah's huff of laughter acknowledged her twin's insight. "I do have something to say, but it can wait until you finish your story. What did Matron say next?"

Charlotte waved off her own punchline with an impatient gesture. "I made my point, darling, as I'm sure you already knew. Matron knows she must rethink her opinions on the superfluity of mathematics for a child from the slums, even those who are as brilliant as young Tony Tweedy. Either that, or she will be seeking another position." She waved an expansive hand. "The stage is yours, Lady Sarah."

Now that the moment had come, Sarah wasn't sure which of

her rehearsed approaches to take. No. This was Charlotte. They might be different in appearance, temperament and interests, but Charlotte was her other self. The persuasive techniques she had learned to manage slum lords and society ladies had no place here.

"I wish to marry," she said, bluntly.

Charlotte's eyes widened. "I did not know you had met anyone you favoured."

Sarah shook her head. "I have not." She leaned across the space between their chairs and took her sister's hand. "I want Elias to have a father and a place in Society, Charlotte. I want..." She looked at her hands. "I want him to have brothers and sisters. I want what cousin Sophia has—to hold my own new born baby in my arms..." Her voice trailed off.

Charlotte squeezed her hand. "I understand. And I suppose the latest family news made it worse."

Sarah nodded. The first time she had seen Jamie's and Sophia's new little girl—cuddled in the arms of her mother with her father hovering, unable to take his proud and doting eyes from the pair of them—she had wanted a painter to capture that moment. Perfect love. The kind of family Uncle James's children had apparently enjoyed, but that she and Sarah had never known. Since then, she had been yearning to be one of the chief actors in her own family portrait.

Not that she was unhappy with Elias. Her little boy was the sweetest and cleverest child in the world. One of the worst things about London was that the hours they enjoyed together in Oxford-shire were diminished to minutes here and there through the day in the townhouse's nursery.

But she wanted more.

The determination that had been growing for months had recently been fuelled when she discovered that Sophia expected to present Jamie with another child later this year, and that cousin Ruth, married nine months ago to the Earl of Ashbury, was already expecting an interesting addition.

"It will have to be the right sort of person. And even if you find someone who will become father to your son and keep your secret, people will talk," Charlotte warned.

Sarah shrugged. "As Uncle James says, people can talk all they like, but if they can't prove anything, and if the leaders of Society accept him, the scandal will disappear."

There would be difficulties, finding someone the chief among them. The right person needed to be tolerant, supportive, respectful of women, understanding of a youthful mistake with consequences. *If I am unable to find such a paragon in Society, I will have to look outside.*

Even once she discovered suitable candidates, she would need to audition them very carefully. If they refused what she asked of them, she could not marry them. After that, their silence and their co-operation would be imperative.

"Darling, what of Nate?" Charlotte asked.

"I have to believe he is dead," Sarah said. "He has been gone seven years, Charlotte. In all that time, he has never tried to contact me. If he is still alive, he doesn't want me. Elfingham said he took money to leave me, and at first I thought he lied, but seven years, Charlotte!"

Charlotte nodded. She, more than anyone, knew that their brother had been unreliable. "Very well," Charlotte said, settling herself back on her cushions and picking up her pen and the pad of paper on which she had been making notes. "Let us make a plan."

2

———————

In the end, Nate didn't head off to London the next morning. When he went up to the nursery to say farewell to his little half-sisters, his stepmother was thrilled to hear he was intending to sample the Marriage Mart. He made no mention of Sarah Winderfield, because he didn't want his father casting any caltrops in his way.

Lady Lechton took his arm and left the nursery with him, rattling away as they walked with a list of reasons why he could not go straight away or alone.

"You will need somewhere to stay—an appropriate address is essential. New clothes, Nate."

Nate was only half listening, but he curbed his impatience to be off. It had taken him a fortnight to convince the timid lady to call him Nate, and he'd no wish to frighten her by cutting her conversation short.

"You dress for comfort," she continued, "which is all very well here in the country, but will not do in Town. Introductions to the proper people, people who will send you invitations. That's very important, Nate. They will be pleased to have you, I can assure you, once they know you are eligible. Young men are much in demand, and handsome young men who are in line for a title… well."

She frowned a little, opened her mouth, shot a nervous look at Nate, and closed it again.

"Go on, Libby," he encouraged her. "What terrible flaw have you noticed that I must needs amend to be acceptable to a suitable lady?"

"Well…" She chewed on her lower lip, examining him with anxious eyes. "You have not been much in Society, Nate," she offered, eventually.

Nate was trying to work out what she was driving at when his father spoke from the door to what he misleadingly called his study —a room in which he drank brandy and slept in front of the fire. "She's right, for once. You are too free and easy, Bentham. You've no idea how to go on in the *Beau Monde*. And you don't have the right connections. No friends from school or that sort of thing."

No, because his father had tutored him at home, reneged on the promise to send him to Oxford in order to keep him as an unpaid secretary, and then when the Duke of Winshire had him abducted, signed him over to the untender mercies of the navy.

"I was at school with some of Society's important hostesses, Lechton," Libby said, her soft voice meek and apologetic. "If we were to go to London with Lord Bentham—"

Lord Lechton interrupted her with a rude snort. "I see your game," he told his wife, scowling. "You think to jaunt up to Town, do you? And spend my money on fripperies, I suppose." He began to shake his head, and Nate spoke quickly, before the old tyrant refused Libby what she clearly saw as a treat. Once he'd spoken, he'd not renege. So much for escaping his father's presence. *Libby's case is worse than mine.* She was stuck with the man until death did them part.

Nate smiled broadly. "What an excellent idea, Libby. Using your connections, I should soon have invitations to places I can meet my future bride, and I'm sure you can counsel me on my manners and dress, too."

Lechton was purpling. Time to apply a little flattery. No, a lot of flattery—applying it with a shovel rather than a trowel would be no more than the earl considered his due. Nor would he note the barb Nate buried in the compliment.

"My lord, I know you will agree, for you have mentioned her ladyship's useful connections to me before. What great foresight you showed in choosing a bride who could be of such assistance to your heir, especially since I was unable to complete my own education as a gentleman."

The earl's scowl deepened. For a moment, Nate thought he had misjudged Lechton's acuity, so he was relieved rather than annoyed when the earl grumbled, "You'd be married already, and likely have given me a grandson by now, if you'd paid more attention to your duties and less to making up to that girl. Instead, here you are, barely more than a savage, and now I have to go to the expense of a London Season for a woman who can't even give me sons. You are a great disappointment to me, Bentham. Beyond a doubt I need to go to London to make sure you don't marry to disoblige me."

He turned his glower on Libby. "Lady Lechton, you shall need to dress to reflect credit on me. You shall have a strict budget, and I shall expect an accounting."

Libby was glowing. Nate had considered her a dowdy sort of a creature, but her delight at the thought of a Season in London made her almost pretty. "Oh, yes, my lord. I shall be most prudent, my lord. You are very kind, my lord." Three 'my lord's' in a row, and nary a mention that the money with which Lechton planned to be parsimonious had come from Libby's dowry. Not for the first time, Nate wondered what had made Libby and her family accept the much older and poorer Earl of Lechton as a suitor. Lust for a title? If so, she was paying a heavy price, poor lady.

He shrugged the mystery off. None of his business, but if he could make Libby's burden a little lighter, he would do it. "When shall we leave, then?" he asked, and resigned himself to the wait when Lord Lechton decreed another week to allow the townhouse in London to be opened, and to prepare to move the entire house-hold, nursery, servants and all.

The twin's list grew through November. Society was greeting those returning to the capital as Parliament began its sessions after the summer recess. Sarah and Charlotte attended entertainments carefully chosen to meet as many suitable gentlemen as possible. After each event, they added names, though they also crossed some out. They wrote notations against every potential candidate they encountered.

"Hythe is probably not ready to set up his nursery," Sarah said, after meeting the earl in question at a dinner party. She wrote this next to his name. That done, *probably* was not *certainly*. He stayed on the list.

"Aldridge probably is ready to set up his nursery," Charlotte noted. The cross through Aldridge's name had been the subject of some debate. The twins agreed that the Duke of Haverford's terminal illness meant his heir, the Marquis of Aldridge, must be in need of a bride, but otherwise disputed his suitability for Sarah.

Charlotte argued that Sarah was not seeking a love match, and that Aldridge met all her specifications for a husband. "He would be a kind, courteous, and respectful husband, Sarah. He is not out for your money or your social position—he has more than enough of both. You get on well with his mother. And they have so much scandal of their own that they're hardly likely to cavil at yours."

Sarah countered with all of the marquis's well-known character flaws, and then won the argument with a sneak attack. "Besides, while I do not want a husband who loves me, nor do I want one who has been dangling after my sister these past four years. He wants you, Charlotte, not me. Besides, even if I was prepared for the embarrassment of being married to a man who loves my sister, I doubt if Aldridge is going to accept such a substitution."

Charlotte shook her head. "It is not love. It can't be. I appear to be a suitable bride for a man of his rank. That is all. But I am not, Sarah. You know I am not."

"I know nothing of the kind." Sarah enfolded her sister in an embrace. "I shall not hound you, my love. But neither shall I marry Aldridge."

Someone would. It should be Charlotte, but Sarah understood the reasons for her sister's reservations, and would say no more. "What of Lord Colyford?" she asked. "I have no objection to a widower, and I have seen his little girls at the park. They appear delightful."

"I'll put him on the list," Charlotte agreed. "Hurley? He seems pleasant enough."

"He can go on the list," Sarah decided, "but I remain to be convinced he has substance to go with his charm."

They added a couple more names and crossed out that of a man who had over-imbibed at Lady Forrest's musical evening. Apparently, he was developing a reputation for becoming drunk and assaulting the maids.

"What are you planning to wear tonight?" Charlotte asked.

"I thought my blue satin-striped sarsenet with the Vandyke lace collar and cuffs."

Charlotte nodded. "That will go well with my green and white muslin with the satin trim."

The sisters usually co-ordinated their toilettes. They were well aware of managing the impact they made together. Since their cousins Ruth and Rosemary arrived in time for the 1812 Spring Season, the four of them had appeared as an ensemble: colours, designs and fabrics carefully chosen so that each complemented the others.

They had been a sensation. Some wit had dubbed them the Four Winds—an obvious allusion to their shared surname, and the foolish swains of Society made a fashion of declaring for one Wind or another, and plying her with compliments, flowers, and charm. Nothing serious. Just frivolous fun. Sarah and Charlotte had not been looking for husbands, and Ruth and Rosemary had their mixed-blood as a counter-weight to their status as daughters to a duke and their generous dowries.

Ruth had found love last year, but not in London. With her marriage just after Christmas, they were down to three remaining

Winds. Two, at the moment, since Rosemary was still in the country, and had no plans to join them until the early Spring next year. What would the wits make of that?

Tonight was another dinner, with cards, music, and perhaps a little dancing after. "We should send for our maids," Sarah suggested. "Drew is escorting us, which is good of him. We should not keep him waiting." Their cousin Drew and their uncle, the Duke of Winshire, were the only other members of the family in Town so far. Drew declared himself happy to play escort. Truly, though, the two of them only needed one another. They had never had the chance to be wide-eyed debutantes, and had reached their majority two years ago.

Indeed, they might be considered at their last prayers, except they were nieces of a duke and well-dowered. Sarah wondered if word was out that she was ready to consider offers for her hand. Perhaps she should mention it in confidence to a couple of well-known gossips.

No. Given her specific requirements, she would continue on the course she and Charlotte had chosen.

"You make a start, darling," she told her sister. "I shall just pop up to the nursery to kiss Elias goodnight. I shall miss him so when we leave for the house party. We have not been apart for a whole week since he came to live with me in April, and the house party will last two."

"It is for a good cause, Sarah. Three of your top contenders will be in residence."

Sarah agreed that the house party would be ideal for getting to know three of her suitors in a relaxed atmosphere. They all appeared to be nice men, and if she had no particular enthusiasm for any one of them, the fault lay with her, surely. Her capacity to love, to even feel desire, had been destroyed before she even made her debut.

She had to keep reminding herself that the goal was worth the sacrifice of her time and energy. This whole husband hunt was tedious, and she'd be glad when it was over and she could get down to being as good a wife as she could manage, and a loving and committed mother.

November was half over before the Lechtons were settled in London, in a townhouse not quite in the best part of town, with opulent public rooms, dowdy private chambers and spartan appointments in the servants' quarters and the utility areas.

As expected, Lechton disappeared to his club, after instructing his wife not to overspend the meagre budget she had been allowed to refurbish her wardrobe. But when Nate offered to remonstrate with the old pinchpenny, Libby stopped him.

"Oh no, Nate. I know just what to do, you'll see. Now, you take down these addresses and go and order your own new clothes."

Nate obeyed orders, though he drew the line when the artists she sent him to tried to impose extremes of fashion on him. He wanted a collar that would allow him to turn his head, and a jacket that did not take three men to pour him into.

Libby demanded he display his purchases, and was pleased to approve them, assuring him she did not expect him to be part of the dandy set.

Meanwhile, after an excursion to an emporium that sold fabric and trimmings, Libby and her maid managed to turn out several ensembles that even Nate could see were very becoming. And when he escorted her two afternoons later to leave her card at the homes of the ladies she remembered from school, several of them were pleased to receive an old friend. More than one asked how she managed to turn out dressed in the height of fashion when she had been mouldering in the wilds of Oxfordshire.

The visits that day and the next achieved all that Nate could hope for. As Libby predicted, an earl's heir without a wife and with all his wits and his teeth could depend upon a steady stream of invitations, even if he was quietly dressed and a little rough around the edges.

Furthermore, without even being prompted, Libby asked who

was in London, and who might be expected to be holding entertainments. Nate listened closely, but when the Duke of Winshire was mentioned, it was only to say that the ducal family had not yet arrived in Town.

Nate had been foolish to hope that he would find Sarah this first week. *Just as well to have time to practice my Society manners and find my feet in her world,* he consoled himself.

With that in mind, he dressed carefully for his first dinner invitation. He was escorting Libby yet again; the Earl having eschewed the event in favour of 'an evening with friends'. Since the man didn't gamble and barely drank, Nate wondered if he had found a mistress. The man claimed to be moral, but he in every other way aped the fashionable elite. Either a mistress, or he preferred the company of his cronies at his club.

Nate wasn't sure whether to pity Libby or to be glad she could enjoy the evening without the censorious presence of her lord and master. "You look lovely this evening," he told her, as she joined him in the foyer.

His father's wife glowed with pleasure. "And you look very fine yourself, Bentham," she replied.

He bowed and offered his elbow. "Madam, your carriage awaits."

"I am so looking forward to this evening, Nate. Perhaps tonight you might meet the young lady who will be your wife!"

Nate smiled and nodded, keeping his reservations to himself. *Not unless my Sarah is present. But she is not yet in town, so it won't be tonight.* And even if she was in town, she would surely not be visiting the Hamners. Lady Hamner had been a ward of the Duchess of Haverford, and—according to Libby—the Dukes of Haverford and Winshire had been feuding since Winshire arrived back in the country with a whole quiverful of foreign-born children.

He allowed daydreams about their next meeting to while away the carriage ride and the wait in the street for other carriages to move out of the way. Libby continued to chatter, but she seldom required a response beyond 'Is that right' and 'If you say so'.

It must have been a good thirty minutes before they were

announced by Lord and Lady Hamner's butler. Libby led him over to the Hamners to be introduced, and Nate looked around as he crossed the room.

A profile caught his eye. He shrugged it off. He had seen Sarah wherever he went for the past seven years, and a closer look always disclosed a stranger. This stranger turned towards him, and he stopped in his tracks, cataloguing changes. The fair hair was slightly darker. The heart-shaped face he remembered had matured into a perfect oval. The slender body of the long-remembered girl had ripened to fulfil its promise. But, beyond any doubt, Lady Sarah Winderfield stood on the other side of the drawing room, a smile on her lips as she talked with her friends.

Her gaze turned towards him just as Libby tugged on his arm. "Bentham! Are you well?" He let her pull him along, and Sarah's gaze drifted away. He wanted to cross the room to her; accost her; demand that she recognise him and all they'd once meant to one another.

Some modicum of sense kept him stumbling after his step-mother. *Men change between seventeen and twenty-four*, he reminded himself. *And people who have been through experiences like mine more than most.*

Still, of all the meetings he'd imagined, he'd never envisaged one in which she didn't know him.

3

———

It was Nate. Sarah kept assuring herself she must be wrong. He had changed so much from the slim boy she had once loved. She smiled and nodded, allowed Lord Hythe to escort her around the room, and made cheerful nonconsequential comments. And all the time, she was conscious of the man, watching him out of the corner of her eye, wondering what it was about him that screamed his identity.

He was a lot taller and broader; that was to be expected. He had been shooting up like a weed when she knew him, but had not yet reached his adult size. His face had squared off. Once, he had been a beautiful youth—a dark-haired Ganymede, her brother called him, with a smirk she didn't understand until her aunt explained that the Trojan prince had been stolen by Zeus who desired him because of his beauty.

Poseidon would fit him better than Ganymede, now. Strength, barely leashed power, serious and forbidding, except when he smiled at the woman with him. Who was she? His wife? They knew one another well, staying within reach of one another as they moved around the room.

She must have money, for she is not beautiful. Sarah scolded herself for the pettiness of the thought. The anger she felt, the pain, all of it should be aimed at Nate, not at some poor female he had charmed with his lies. If they were lies.

He was breath-taking when stern. Then his companion made a remark that brought a curve to his lips and the smile transformed him. Even the scar that crossed one cheek in a ragged line added to his beauty, a contrast to perfection.

The eyes were the same, she decided. The same colour and shape, at least, though the cynicism with which he regarded the company was new.

Before they had reached the group that included Sarah, Hamner's butler called dinner, and Lady Hamner began pairing people off to go to the dining table. Nate, Sarah noticed, was paired with another lady, and the one he had arrived with happily accepted the escort of one of the lords Sarah had on her list.

Charlotte guided her own dinner partner over to Sarah, and asked, out of the corner of her mouth, "What is the matter?" Her twin might not know what was wrong, but she always knew how Sarah felt.

"No time. Can we go straight home after dinner?" Sarah whispered back. The line passed through the doorway, and the sisters had to peel off in different directions, but Charlotte would make their excuses when the time came. Sarah couldn't face Nate until she had time to absorb the fact of his return.

In the half-light just before dawn, the last of the club's patrons stumbled out of the front door, those employees who did not reside in their place of work left through the back door, and the building slipped into its usual early morning slumber.

The club comprised two houses thrown into one in a street of four-story terraced houses. Behind, the areas that serviced the public rooms and accommodated the owners and their employees had spread to include the building's neighbours in the parallel street, but that was not obvious from the front. There, apart from its double width, little set the building apart from its neighbours. Perhaps it was a little tidier; its window-sills and doors newly painted, its bricks scrubbed and firmly set in newly pointed mortar. Only the discreet brass sign beside the door identified it as very different from the family homes and boarding houses that surrounded it.

Heaven and Hell, the sign whispered, engraved into the brass in discrete italics, only an inch tall. To read it at all, even in the light of the lamp that had hung just above it all night, one needed to climb the steps from the street. No one came to the building without a personal referral, but occasionally, first-time visitors needed reassurance that they were in the right place before they were emboldened to knock on the door.

A glimpse through the open door as the porter allowed entry would leave a passer-by with an impression of light and gilt. Members, or those referred by members, were surrounded by opulence as soon as they stepped inside. Opulence and decadence. In Heaven and Hell, nothing was forbidden. Everything was available for a price.

The woman known as La Reine, the ruler of the brothel Heaven that occupied the two upper floors of the main house, retired to her personal sitting room in a penthouse suite above the mean street behind the club. It had been a profitable night in her realm. Supper was laid ready in the dining room she shared with her business partner. When he joined her, she would find out how things went in Hell, the gambling establishment on the lower two floors.

"Are you coming to bed, my Queen?" The youth lounged in the doorway to her bedchamber, one bare leg splitting the silk robe that was knotted at his waist with a deliberate negligence that left most of his chest bare.

La Reine scanned him with her eyes, lingering on the groin where her favourite attribute was swelling at her attention, tenting the silk. He half lowered his eyelids and pursed his lips in a kiss. La Reine smiled. She had auditioned several of the lads who served those with an appetite for such things, but had chosen to keep this one after the first time she took him to her bed, for his enthusiastic application to her pleasure and his own.

"Not yet, kitten. I have business to attend to, first." The reluctance in her voice was genuine. Observing others at their pleasure always left her wet and ready for her own.

Kit pouted. "Do you have to see *him*?"

His jealousy was probably feigned, but he did it well, and it pleased her to pretend that he resented the time she spent with The Beast, her business partner. Still, he had no right to question her, or to comment on her decisions.

"Go to bed, Kitten. I will wake you if you are asleep when I join you." With a final pout, a flounce, and a wiggle of his rather fine buttocks, he obeyed, closing the door behind him.

She could set him at ease with a word, but no one knew that The Beast was her brother, nor would they. Those who knew her from her previous life as Countess of Ashbury saw only the costume she wore as La Reine; those who might remember her brother would never see the Duke of Devil's Kitchen or that runaway felon Stanley Wharton in the golden goat's mask of The Beast and the red locks she dyed in the privacy of his chambers every Sunday afternoon.

In the carriage with Drew, Charlotte kept up a light chatter to distract their cousin from Sarah's pallor and silence. It didn't work, but he accepted the excuse of a megrim, and wished the sisters a good night's sleep before leaving them at the Winshire mansion, and heading out to find entertainment elsewhere.

In their rooms, Charlotte sent the waiting maids away. "My sister and I will look after ourselves this evening." She waited until the door closed, leaving them alone.

"He is Viscount Bentham, heir to the Earl of Lechton. The lady he escorted tonight is Lady Lechton, his father's wife," she reported, as she began to undo the fastenings on the side of Sarah's gown. "Apparently, Mr Beauclair inherited about five years ago, after the deaths of those in direct line. I was sitting next to Lord Farnham tonight, and he was on the Committee of Privileges when he was confirmed."

"I don't know Lady Lechton," Sarah commented, "though she looked to be our age or a little older. She wasn't out in London when we were."

"She's from a wealthy merchant family. Turn around, dearest, and let me loosen your waist string." Charlotte busied her fingers in the ribbon, which had become knotted. "Birmingham, Farnham thinks. She had a very large dowry, and traded it for a title. Poor thing."

Sarah almost didn't want to ask. Had Nate been in England all this time? She had grieved to think him dead, raged at the idea he might have taken her father's money and run away overseas. But she had never imagined that the man she had once loved lived within a few days' ride of her.

As usual, Charlotte understood what she was thinking, and answered without waiting for the question. "Farnham says that the Privileges Committee was told that Lechton's son was dead. Then, two months ago, Lechton wrote to say it had all been a mistake. The young man had been found and was back with his family."

"If even his family thought he was dead…" Sarah was finally able to slide her gown off her shoulders and let it slip to the floor.

Charlotte grimaced. "Who knows? Farnham also pointed out that Lady Lechton has three daughters, and rumour has it she is not able to have another child."

Sarah stepped out of her gown, picked it up, and folded it over the back of a chair. "Turn around, Charlotte," she commanded, and began the task of unhooking her sister. "How did your part of the table react to your interest in the Lechtons?"

Charlotte shrugged. "I did not have to ask a single question. Apparently, Bentham is the *topic du jour*. Some of the men have met him out making calls with his stepmother. He has apparently been in the navy, most recently as a student physician at the university in Edinburgh."

Sarah raised her brows. The navy? He had never mentioned any interest in becoming a sailor. "Ready," she said to her sister, and helped her lift her gown over her head.

"Sit down, sweetheart, and I shall brush your hair," Charlotte offered.

Sarah watched her sister's face in the mirror. She knew that look. "Out with it, Charlotte. What are you not telling me?"

"Lechton has told the men at his club that he has brought Bentham to London to choose a bride."

Charlotte's hands stilled for a moment, then she resumed the soothing motion of the brush until Sarah spun on the chair to face her. "Shouldn't you tell him, Sarah? Doesn't he have a right to know?"

Sarah shook her head. "He wasn't there, Charlotte. He left, with never a word. I've not heard from him from that day to this." She rose and stepped away.

Charlotte followed her, and wrapped her arms around her. "I know," she murmured. "I know."

Sarah held herself stiff for a moment, then relaxed into her sister's embrace. "I can't face him, Charlotte. Not yet."

"When you are ready," Charlotte agreed. "You need to know what really happened, Sarah, or you'll always wonder."

Charlotte had the right of it. She was a bubbling stew of anger, longing and old sorrow. But underneath lurked the need to know for certain whether Nate had lied to get her into his bed; whether he had seduced and abandoned her, and if so, whether he had meant to do so all along.

Underneath the ferment, the thread of hope she'd never quite surrendered whispered that perhaps he had intended to be true. Perhaps he had been coerced in some way. Unlikely. If so, why had he not written? Why had he not returned to her when he came back to Great Britain?

Still, she would give him his chance. "After the house party," she told Charlotte. "Time enough to arrange to meet him when I return. I will leave for Lady de Witt's tomorrow morning, a day early, before he has a chance to call. *If* he intends to call. If Drew cannot escort me, he can wait and come with you. I can make the trip before dark and will be safe with the outriders."

And she would take Elias with her. Lady de Witt would not mind, and Elias would enjoy being in the company of other children. The risk that Nate would hear about her ward was low, and even if he did, he'd hear the manufactured story that Elias was the by-blow of one of the deceased Winderfield men, either Sarah's brother or her father. It was unlikely in the extreme that he'd guess the carefully hidden truth.

Still, Sarah would feel safer if Elias was within reach of her arms.

4

Nate waited impatiently for the hour past noon, the earliest he could possibly make a call to the Winderfield household. Libby planned to begin her courtesy calls at three of the clock. "Even that is early, Nate."

"I will arrive in time to escort you, Libby," he promised.

However, the formidable butler at the Winshire mansion shook his head at Nate's request to have his card taken to Lady Sarah. "I regret, sir, that Lady Sarah is not in residence."

Nate fought the inclination to point out he had seen the lady only the previous evening. If she had told the Winshire butler to deny him entry, any arguments he might make would be met with a blandly polite wall of repudiation.

The butler, though, did not leave it at that. He unbent enough to say, "Lady Sarah left for the country this morning, my lord."

Nate knew it was no use, but he asked anyway, where she had gone and how long she would be away.

As expected, the butler refused to answer. "It is not my place to say, sir."

Nate was turning away when he had another thought. The butler had said Lady Sarah had left. "Perhaps you could take my card up to Lady Charlotte? Tell her I would be grateful if she could spare me a moment of her time."

He more than half expected the butler to explain that Lady Charlotte was also out of town. However, the man merely bowed, and asked him to wait. He ushered Nate into a small parlour, and carried off the card.

Nate tried to remember what Lady Charlotte was like. He had barely noticed her yesterday evening, his attention all on not embarrassing Lady Sarah or, for that matter, Libby, by staring at his long-lost love like a gawky youth. He had a vague impression she was much of a size with her sister, but brown-haired where Sarah was fair.

In that golden summer when he and Sarah had become friends and then more, Charlotte had been ill with some embarrassing childhood illness; mumps, he thought. Sarah—at a loose end without her twin—had wandered the estate and come across the vicar's son in the woods, rescuing a rabbit from a trap.

Nate had met Charlotte once. She insisted on a meeting before she agreed to cover for her sister while Nate and Sarah eloped. He must have passed muster, but he had few memories of the encounter. At the time, thoughts of Sarah had filled his every waking moment and fuelled his dreams. When he was with her, he was blind to everything else.

He knew Charlotte the girl through Sarah's descriptions. Loving, loyal, the best friend a sister could have. Those would still be true after seven years, surely? If she would talk to him, he could, perhaps, find out what he most needed to know.

"Lord Bentham. Have we met, sir?"

Nate spun round to face the lady who had just entered the room. A maid crept in behind her and took station in the corner, but Nate's full attention was for Lady Charlotte. She was similar in size and build to Sarah, but on the surface, little else was the same. Except that, as she tilted her head to the side to study him as he was examining her, the gesture and her thoughtful expression brought powerful memories rushing back.

"She used to look at me like that when she was irritated with me," he blurted.

Some of the tension went out of Lady Charlotte's shoulders, and one corner of her mouth twitched as if she suppressed a smile. "She, so our old governess used to say, is the cat's mother."

Nate felt his cheeks heat. "Lady Sarah, I mean. I beg your pardon. And yes, we have met, though it was many years ago."

Lady Charlotte considered him a moment longer, then waved to a group of chairs set around a low table. "Sit down, Lord Bentham. Tell me what brings you here."

The answer was the same two words. "Lady Sarah." Nate had so many questions he wanted to ask that he couldn't think what to say first.

Lady Charlotte spoke before he could. "My sister is in the country. She is seeking a husband this Season, and hopes to narrow her shortlist."

A shortlist of potential husbands? The room spun for a moment and Nate spoke before his brain connected with his tongue. "Me! She doesn't need another husband." Lady Charlotte raised her brows at him, and he realised he was shouting. He lowered his voice, but he couldn't retract anything he had said. "Just me."

"You." Lady Charlotte's scorn dripped from the word in edged icicles. "You left, seven years ago, without goodbyes."

"Not of my own volition," Nate protested.

Lady Charlotte's nostrils flared, but she commented only, "For seven years? And not a single word, then or later?"

Sarah did not receive any of my letters! Nate forced his fists to relax. "I wrote."

"Not a word," Lady Charlotte repeated, raising an eyebrow.

The lady has a right to her doubts. And Sarah, too, if she in truth heard nothing from me.

"I owe *Lady Sarah* an explanation, my lady," he said, hoping his voice sounded much calmer than he felt. "I hope to have the opportunity to give it to her."

Lady Charlotte surprised him with a wry smile. "You do not owe me an explanation, you mean."

That was exactly what he meant. He couldn't resist a smile of his own. "Your sister said you were smart."

She folded her hands in her lap, composing herself back into the model of an ice maiden she had appeared at the outset. "Very well, my lord. I am to join my sister in a couple of days. We shall be back in town in two weeks. She will decide whether or not to give you a hearing once we return, but I will tell her everything you have said."

"But what if…?" Nate had been about to ask whether Lady Sarah was going to choose a husband before he could see her again. *Narrow the shortlist, she said. I still have time.*

His thoughts must have shown on his face, for Lady Charlotte said, "I do not expect my sister to be betrothed when she returns to London, if that is what bothers you."

Nate couldn't deny her point but didn't want to give her the satisfaction of knowing she had him to rights. He bowed instead. "Thank you for seeing me today, my lady."

It was a polite nothing masking his irritation that she had told him very little, and by the twinkle in her eye, she knew it. *Sarah is choosing a husband.* That thought dominated all others, and he had been escorted to the door by a footman and was out on the street again before he was fully aware of being dismissed.

His childhood sweetheart, his first love, was planning to choose a husband. His reaction—the sheer revulsion at the thought of her with anyone else—had been unexpected. Yes, he had wanted to meet her again, let her know what had happened to him, make peace between them.

He had planned to do whatever was needed to resolve any difficulties their past actions might make for her future. He had even hoped to find out whether the grown Sarah and the grown Nate might be able to find some sparks of the fire that once burned when they touched.

Nearly a third of my life has passed, and I have changed. She must have, too. Perhaps they would meet and dislike one another, or meet and agree to part as friends. But his immediate reaction when Lady Charlotte mentioned that damnable list was to claim his long-lost love as his own.

Nate had walked seven blocks and had passed the street he was meant to turn down. He backtracked to the missed corner. *Nothing has changed. Everything has changed.* He still could not move on with his own life until he knew whether the unbroken connection between him and Sarah Winderfield was all on his side, or whether she felt it too. *But the clock is ticking. She means to take a husband!*

He needed to meet Sarah, clear up her misconceptions about his disappearance and presumed silence, find out if he still wanted the role that had once been his greatest ambition, and convince her to love him again. And all before she chose another husband.

A thought occurred and stopped him short. She had a shortlist. *I am not competing against a love match.* He stepped out towards his father's townhouse, a smile spreading as he considered that fact. He'd put the next two weeks to good use, using Libby and her contacts to find out who was courting Lady Sarah, who she favoured, and what they were like.

The clubs, too. He'd buy horses and play cards—whatever it took to be accepted into the conversation men had when women were not around. *By the time I see her again, I'll be armed for the battle ahead.* He'd know what she looked for in a husband, and also what was wrong with the suitors she was considering.

Nate found that Sarah's interest in finally choosing a husband had attracted attention. It fascinated the bored young men who inhabited the clubs, moved in packs to entertainments in both high and low society, and whiled away their hours by wagering, gossiping, and competing within their set: Corinthians, Dandies, Young Blades, Peep-O-Day Boys.

"The Winderfield Diamond?" said one rakish gentleman, when Nate managed to bring her name into a conversation over brandy. "Nothing there. She looks lovely, I'll grant you, but not safe. Even before those terrifying cousins arrived, a man 'd risk his future offspring getting too close. Seems very sweet, right up until she freezes you into an ice block."

"And her sister!" His friend shuddered. "Cut you into little strips with her tongue, that one."

"Anyway," Rake One commented, "she's looking for a groom. Don't know why this season, when she's turned down more proposals than any other female on the Marriage Mart. Truth to tell, I only chanced my arm because of that. I usually leave the virgins alone, but I thought she'd decided on spinsterhood."

"Anyone would have," his friend commiserated. "Did myself." He shook his head. "Doesn't like men."

"Then why is she getting married?" the first rake asked.

They considered the perplexing conundrum of a woman who did not find their advances appealing while Nate thought about how satisfying it would be to punch them.

Someone sitting nearby interrupted their silence. "Bit of a honey pot all around. Looks, money, connections. A man could do worse. And if she doesn't warm up in bed, that's what mistresses are for."

"Good luck with that," another opined. "She's already turned away don't-know-how-many fortune hunters. The war office should hire her mother and her aunt. Their intelligence gathering is unbelievable."

The topic drifted and circled, but kept coming back to what gossip had gleaned about Sarah's intentions and expectations. Nate didn't have to say a word. He sat and sipped his brandy, and before an hour had passed, he had a list of eight men that, the company agreed, the Winderfield Diamond was considering.

Other conversations added two more, and rounded out a picture of a settled man with interests beyond fashion, gambling, and sports. Of the seven landowners, four were peers and three untitled gentlemen. The three younger sons all had independent incomes from their own successful enterprises, one as a Member of Parliament in Commons, one an architect, and one a barrister. Nine of the ten preferred country to London living. Four were widowers, two with children.

One factor they had in common was that all had a name as philanthropists, in some measure. That was another thing Nate learned about the Winderfield family in general and Sarah and her twin in particular. They not only supported good causes, they actively worked in charitable ventures as diverse as barefoot schools, orphanages, and support for military widows and their children.

Most of the useless fribbles who gossiped in his hearing were contemptuous of such efforts. "Not going to be able to make silk out of that kind of sow's ear." The young viscount expressing that opinion was only saying what his fellows thought. "Those who are born in the gutter belong there. Don't have the brains for anything else, and will rob you soon as look at you."

Nate kept to his corner and sipped his drink. What would these idiots say if they knew where he was heading tomorrow? Out of curiosity, he had walked past the ragged school that Lady Charlotte not only sponsored but taught in. In an adjoining street, he had seen a medical clinic that offered care to anyone who came. On an impulse, he had gone in, introduced himself, and asked for a tour.

They'd been in the process of politely refusing when several people were carried in from the street in fast succession, bruised, broken and bleeding from an encounter with a runaway dray. "Let me help," Nate had offered to the harried doctor who came hurrying down from upstairs in his shirtsleeves.

He'd been grilled about his experience and training in between terse commands to hold this, pass that, and tie the other thing. "You know what you're doing," the doctor conceded after they'd passed quickly down the line of patients, checking breathing and bleeding and providing immediate emergency care. "Carry on. You take the big man with the broken femur. I'll sew up the split eyebrow."

An hour later—the ambulatory on their way home, the remaining two who needed overnight medical supervision in beds in a clean ward upstairs—they finally introduced themselves. "Nate Beauclair," Nate said. His courtesy title would only get in the way. "Late of Edinburgh University, where I read medicine, and before that, apprentice to a ship's surgeon in the Royal Navy."

The other doctor grasped the hand Nate offered. "I'm Blythe, the resident physician here. We have others who come in on regular clinic days: Tuesday, Thursday, and Saturday. Even the founder, when she is in town. Cup of tea?"

Nate nodded his agreement, and Blythe led the way across the hall that divided the upper floor into two halves. He unlocked a door and showed Nate into a comfortable sitting room. "My apartment—comes with the residency. Are you looking for a job, Beauclair?"

He busied himself with stirring up the fire and moving a kettle close to the flame. "I'll warn you, mine is the only paid position. Most of our doctors are volunteers."

Nate passed him the tin of tea that perched on the mantlepiece. "I already have a position, but it is only part time. Do you need another volunteer?"

Blythe measured three spoons of tea into a waiting teapot. "We always need another volunteer. The lines get longer week by week. I've been telling the founder that we should add another clinic day, but we don't have the doctors. If you're serious, I'll put in a word."

Over tea, the conversation turned to their medical training. Blythe had his degree from the University of Oxford, and had finished his study with practical experience at St Bartholomew's in London. Nate had had the practical experience first, and sat the second-year examinations at Edinburgh based on what he'd learned from his shipboard mentor, Dr Macintosh.

It had been Macintosh who had kept him alive and put him back together when he was first thrown aboard ship, and who had taken him on as loblolly boy once he recovered enough to do a few tasks around the hospital room to show his gratitude.

After several years, Macintosh talked the navy into sending him to university to get his qualifications. Nate had just been reassigned to a ship when his father interfered, and the Admiralty, curse them, accepted the argument that the welfare of the kingdom required the earl to have an heir to his estates and title.

Mind you, had they not, he would not have been here, in London, just in time to seize the chance for a future with Sarah, if there was one.

"Come back tomorrow, if you can," Blythe suggested, as they

parted. "It's a clinic day, and you might like to meet some of the others."

Nate agreed. He'd tell Libby that he wouldn't be available for afternoon calls, but he would escort her to the theatre that night. For the first time since leaving Edinburgh, he was looking forward to the next day.

5

───────

After three days at the house party, Sarah was fighting the urge to order her carriage and escape. Charlotte had not arrived, instead sending a message to say that something had come up concerning the school and she would be there as soon as she could.

Some of the more disreputable house guests had taken Charlotte's absence to mean Sarah would be susceptible to their charms, which was more than a little insulting. Jeremy Parkswick was typical. He found her on her own in the stables when she lingered to feed an apple to her mount. "I am pleased to see you here without your twin, lovely Sarah," he said in a husky voice that she presumed she was meant to find appealing.

As if Sarah, without Charlotte, would not have the brains to see that Parkswick was all glitter and no substance! She moved away from the corner to which he was trying to herd her. "And why is that, Mr Parkswick?"

He shifted to block her exit. "I mean no offense, dear lady. Lady Charlotte is very worthy, I suppose. But she is a bluestocking and a prude, and out to spoil a man's fun."

In their first year as debutantes, Society had dubbed Sarah the

Diamond and Charlotte the Saint. They seemed to think Sarah's fashionable colouring and figure were the sum total of her person, and being beautiful must necessarily mean being stupid. Charlotte's preference for a quieter social life and her dedication to educational causes meant, in their eyes, she was some kind of a religious fanatic, determined to spoil their fun.

Parkswick's fun, in this case, fetched him sore toes from Sarah's riding boot. The fool did not take the hint, spreading his legs to move his feet away from her stamp and wrapping her in an embrace that stank of an over-floral cologne, male perspiration, and brandy. "Clumsy, clumsy, my pet. If you want to play, I have some better ideas."

"Release me immediately, Mr Parkswick, or I shall ask my cousin Drew to teach you some manners," Sarah informed him. The threat would provoke less gossip, if a lower degree of personal satisfaction, than a sound punch to his mating equipment.

Drew's marksmanship had become legendary in his first months in England, when he had shot the buttons off an opponent's jacket in a duel, then repeated the feat at Manton's with a succession of volunteers. He was equally skilled with a sword and with his fists. Parkswick let her go and slunk off muttering that he only meant to steal a kiss, and she was as cold as her sister.

Sarah hadn't, in fact, told her cousin. Drew presented as an affable easy-going young man, slow to take offence and always ready with a joke to diffuse a tense situation. But scratch that surface, and the warrior lurked beneath. As her escort, Drew would take any threat to her seriously, and—while Parkswick probably deserved to be thrashed—any such intervention would itself generate gossip. Sarah had no wish to become an object of pity or, for that matter, the villainess of the piece, luring hapless rakes into fights with her formidable relative.

Besides, on their way to the house party, she had asked Drew to give her space to get to know the three gentleman guests who were on her husband shortlist, and she hated to have to admit that was a mistake. *However, if the rakes and scoundrels refuse to take my 'no' for an answer, I shall have to enlist Drew to have a quiet word with them.*

Sarah sighed. Her husband list was shrinking, too. Out of three candidates at this party, two had disqualified themselves already. Drew had taken her aside after dinner on the second day. "Lord Hurley is a dedicated gambler, cousin. Most of the men here will not play with him, as he is falling further and further into debt, and has already sold the estate he inherited and much of his other property. He needs a wealthy wife to fund his habit."

Sarah had no objection to a man marrying her for her dowry, but not if he was likely to wager it away and leave her and Elias penniless.

Lord Colyford had seemed promising. He wanted a wife to mother his little girls and provide a son or two. Since Sarah wanted a father for her son and more children, it would be an even bargain. He was pleasant to talk to, treated her as if her opinions had value, and showed no signs of descending into sentiment. This was to be a practical marriage, with respect and affection certainly, but Sarah had done with love.

The twinge when she thought of Nate was a scarred-over wound, mostly sound but subject to the occasional phantom pain. That was what she had been telling herself, trying not to build anything on the visit her sister had written about, or his expressed desire to explain himself.

Then, yesterday, she had been out for a walk with Colyford and several other guests. They had rounded a hedge and come across the nursery party. Elias had run to meet Sarah, his face alight with pleasure. What a far cry from the nervous little creature Mrs Wakefield had brought her just eight months ago. Sarah returned the child's bow, then crouched to present her cheek for a kiss.

"Ladies, gentlemen, may I make known to you my ward, Master Elias Winderfield?"

Several of the ladies bent for a word with the little boy. Some of the gentleman, too, bestowed a smile on him from their various heights. Not, Sarah noted, Colyford.

"What are you up to today," Jessica Grenford asked Elias. Jessica was one of the Duchess of Haverford's three wards. They were all, though the ton pretended not to notice, base-born daughters of the

Duke of Haverford, and therefore half-sisters to one another and to the Marquis of Aldridge.

Jessica's attention proved too much for Elias, who muttered something unintelligible.

"Oh, he is shy," one of the other ladies cooed. "How sweet."

Sarah stood and claimed the child's hand. "Time to return to nurse, dearest," she suggested, and led Elias a few paces away to where the nurse waited. Another kiss, and the child and nurse rejoined the rest of their group, Elias recovering enough to turn to wave to Sarah.

As they continued on their walk, the ladies chatted about how handsome Elias was, and how sweetly he bowed. "You haven't had him for long, have you?" commented one of the silliest debutantes. "I thought he would be rougher. Because of..." she trailed off, as one of her friends poked her.

Sarah thought it kinder to ignore the remark, and the whispered aside to the helpful friend. "Well, everyone knows that she took him out of a workhouse."

Jessica, bless her, said, "I believe we are to have dancing after tea tonight, and a picnic at the ruins tomorrow, if the weather holds."

The distraction worked, the rest of the party more than happy to talk about their own entertainment rather than the dubious origins of the newest chick in the Winderfield nest. Elias wasn't mentioned again until they were returning to the house. The party had spread out by then, and Sarah was walking on Colyford's arm.

Colyford's voice was stiff and cold when he said, "I had been told that you'd taken guardianship of your brother's er—love child. Or is he your father's?"

Sarah shrugged. Few people had asked her outright, but she had developed an answer that avoided lying. "It does not matter, Lord Colyford. He is a Winderfield, as anyone can see by looking him."

Colyford harrumphed. "I cannot think it suitable, Lady Sarah, an unmarried lady like yourself having charge of a child like that. One would commend the duke for providing appropriate support for such a child, but making the brat the responsibility of a maiden lady is hardly appropriate."

Sarah was finding the man less attractive by the minute. She didn't bother asking him what he meant by 'such a child'; his attitude answered the question. "Elias is *my* ward, Lord Colyford, not my uncle's. *I* 'took him in', as you put it. His Grace has been good enough to support my decision."

Colyford stopped in his tracks and turned to her, so that she had to drop his arm or be indecorously close. He picked up her hands, and gave his most charming smile, softening his voice to coax rather than hector. "Now, my dear, I do not mean to scold you. Of course, at your age, you want a child to care for. That is perfectly understandable. But this is not the way, my lady. You have been poorly advised, I can see. His Grace, while a very good sort of man, does not understand English Society, and who can wonder."

Sarah, struck speechless by the sheer arrogance of the man, did not reply, and hc took her silence as consent, tucking her hand back into his elbow and patting it with his other hand as he led her towards the house.

"You must have noticed that I have been particular in my attentions, Lady Sarah. Or may I call you Sarah, perhaps? I think I have the right to advise you that you must be prepared to give up your ward. Your uncle has the means to keep him, if he so wishes. Indeed, given the example of the Duchess of Haverford, it is a wonder we are not overrun with people of the most shocking origins, all of whom we must treat as if they are worthy of respect. Even marrying among us!"

He chuckled, and patted her hand again, and Sarah contemplated hitting him with it. "Well, Lord Hamner is a fool. The younger Miss Grenford is a better prospect, perhaps. At least we may be permitted to believe her mother to be of a more elevated position, even though of unfortunate morals. And she has been raised as a lady, at least, as has Lady Hamner. They say your little ward was found in a workhouse!

"I must tell you, Lady Sarah, that my wife must be above reproach. I have to think of poor Maria's daughters, but even were that not the case, I could not bring shame upon my name by taking to wife anyone whose virtue could be questioned. Why, those with scurrilous minds are even now suggesting that you would only have taken the little boy in if the relationship was closer than nephew or brother."

Sarah managed to extract her hand. "Lord Colyford, I am appalled by your attitude to an innocent child, one whose birth circumstance can in no way be blamed upon him. I can see that I have been mistaken in thinking we might share similar opinions of matters of importance. I wish you well on your search for a suitable mother for your daughters."

Colyford looked more puzzled than indignant or grieved. "Do try to be reasonable, my dear. The sins of the fathers are visited upon the children. Everyone knows that. I am not blaming the child, but facts are facts, Sarah."

"I have not made you free of my name, my lord," Sarah reminded him.

"Sarah?" It was Drew, striding towards them from the house.

Relieved, Sarah told Colyton, "I have no further need of your escort, Lord Colyton." She swallowed some of her annoyance and added, "Thank you for being honest with me." After all, even if that was two out of three suitors gone, at least she would waste no further time on someone so totally unsuitable to be Elias's new father.

She pushed down the recurring and stupid hope that Nate would seek to be considered for the role. *He left. Disappeared without a word.* Charlotte had told him he'd have the chance to explain, and she would not make her sister foresworn. *I will listen to his excuses, then give him his quittance.* That was the wise course, was it not?

"I will be back in a day or two," His Grace of Winshire told his niece, the only one of the immediate family in residence. Not that he was leaving her unchaperoned or unprotected; quite apart from the English servants, he had assigned several of his personal retainers to the protection of each of his family members.

Still, he was not comfortable leaving Charlotte in London

without himself or one of his sons. His retainers were fiercely loyal warriors, to a man and a woman, but the political and social challenges the Winshires had faced since their return from Central Asia usually didn't lend themselves to solutions at the point of a sword.

Charlotte stood on tiptoes to kiss his cheek. "I have a meeting tomorrow afternoon, Uncle James, and the next day I am joining Sarah and Drew in the country. I will be well escorted, and you are not to worry."

"Don't take any risks, my dear," he begged her. His blood ran cold when he remembered how she used to walk to the boundaries of one of the worst slums in London with no more escort than her maid and an unarmed footman. Of course, the ragged school she had founded, and in which she taught, needed to be close to where its students dwelt.

She was her mother's daughter. Indeed, all of the Winshire womenfolk were actively involved in what his dear departed wife, a devout Christian in the ancient Aramaic Church of Persia, would call the Works of Mercy.

"Yahzak will not allow me to go into danger, Uncle," she pointed out.

Yahzak was commander of her personal guard. A good man. Winshire had shared with Yahzak the latest inconclusive reports that made him so edgy about leaving Charlotte behind in London.

He hadn't told Charlotte, not wanting to alarm her. In the back of his mind, he could hear his wife's dear voice, scolding. Or perhaps it wasn't Mahzad but Eleanor, the Duchess of Haverford and once his dearest love. Both strong-minded women would insist that knowledge was power and ignorance risk. They were right, of course.

"Charlotte, there may be no cause for alarm, but we have reports to suggest that the former Lady Ashbury and her brother did not leave England. Our cousin the Weasel may have been sent off with a couple of decoys to disguise the fact they are still in the country. Possibly in London. When we took Wharton down, we knew another villain would rise to the top. But we now believe that one of the main contenders for mastery in the St Giles slums may be Wharton in a new guise."

Charlotte's eyes widened. Wharton and his sister had carried out several attacks on the Winshires in the past two years, culminating in a kidnap attempt that had ended in a pitched battle where they were defeated and sent for trial. "And Lady Ashbury?"

"If our identification of Wharton is correct—it is currently based on a similarity of physical type and certain unpleasant personal tastes that I will not discuss with a lady—then he runs a gambling hell that is associated with a brothel. The woman in charge of the brothel is always masked. But she could be Lady Ashbury."

He shrugged. It was all conjecture. His investigators were exploring leads, looking for proof.

"Be careful, Charlotte," he said again. "I do not expect trouble. Even if it is them, they are wanted on capital crimes. They would be foolish to attack us again and disclose their identities."

"Hatred can make people stupid, Uncle James," Charlotte said, wisely. "And they hate us. I promise I will be careful."

6

Since all he could do about Lady Sarah was wait for her to return to London, Nate bent his mind to serving in the Ashbury Clinic, and was pleased when an interview concluded with an invitation to volunteer. He contracted to make himself available during the day on two days a week and for one evening, his need to keep his activities secret from his father prohibiting a deeper commitment.

Libby accepted his explanation of a regular commitment without comment. His father assumed he had set up a mistress, and expressed himself pleased that the boy had normal appetites. Nate avoided looking at Libby, who was present for his father's remarks, and managed, he hoped, not to show his disgust.

The thought of being the profligate that his father apparently expected made Nate feel ill. His faithfulness to his first love, at first almost inadvertent, had become an established habit. Despite his conviction that he had lost her, some hope must have remained, for the guilt he felt when he was tempted to stray had been enough to reinforce his virtue. Now, the knowledge that Sarah was alive and unattached—the sight of her, even though she fled from him—these were enough to drown the least morsel of desire for any other woman. His father would not be pleased, but Nate could not consider another wife.

The clinic work was interesting—they saw it all—knife wounds, broken bones, illnesses that swept through the slum. On his first evening on duty, he and the resident doctor, James Blythe, were called out to a woman labouring with child in a small tidy flat on the outskirts of the worst of the slum. "By the time we are called," warned Blythe, "it is usually too late."

This time, though, the father had run for them early when the midwife had turned up too far gone with gin to be of any use. It was not the woman's first child, and it was a relatively straightforward breech presentation. Nate managed to turn the child, leaving the three children she already had with a living mother, provided child-birth fever didn't take her. He stopped the husband in the hallway of the tenement block, as he showed them to the door, and suggested continence, but he didn't need his colleague's muttered remark that it would be of no use.

"You'll do," said Blythe, as they walked back to the clinic. "Don't go into the slums without taking a porter, but you can deal with any other calls tonight on your own. Wake me if you have any problems, but otherwise, I'm for bed when we get back."

Nate nodded, pleased that he'd passed whatever standard Blythe had in mind. "I will." He continued to scan the darkness beyond range of Blythe's lantern. His travels had taken him many places where a moment's inattention in the darkness would get a man killed.

Was that a moan? He hesitated for a moment, and the sound came again—a brief whimper, choked off, as if the sufferer was afraid to make a noise.

On the steps of the building they were passing, in the shadows, a bundle of rags suddenly shifted away from the light, groaning at the effort. Nate took a step closer, one hand on the dagger he carried in his pocket. It must be a person. A small woman or perhaps a child.

Blythe laid a hand on his arm. "Have a care."

"Don't be afraid." Nate addressed the person on the steps. "We are doctors. We want to help you." He took a step closer as Blythe raised the lantern.

The rag bundle lowered the arm behind which it was hiding, and wary hazel eyes glinted in the flickering light.

Nate crouched, just out of arm's reach, his hand still on his dagger. "What's wrong?"

"It's me leg, in't it." The voice was young, and—even though strained with pain—laced with belligerence and bravado. "Me ribs, too. I fell."

Blythe drew nearer, the lantern light showing a thin dirty face covered in scrapes and bruises.

"We need to get him to the clinic," Blythe said. "I'll fetch help. He shouldn't be moved without a stretcher."

He handed Nate the lantern and hurried away.

"We are doctors from the Ashbury clinic," Nate explained. "We'll take you there and have a look at your injuries." Definitely male, from the clothing. It was good quality clothing, too, from what he could see through the dirt. Quality, and little worn.

"Tell my lady?" the boy begged, though speaking clearly pained him. "Tell her Tony din't run. They took me from 'er garden. Tell her?"

A servant of some kind? "Who is your lady, Tony?" Nate asked. "I'll send a message."

"Saint Charlotte. Her wot teaches here."

Surely, he didn't mean Sarah's sister? She was a benefactor of the ragged school on whose steps they stood, but did she actually teach? Before Nate could question the boy, Blythe hurried back with one of the clinic's porters and a collapsible stretcher. They shifted the patient as gently as possible, but he passed out before the transfer was complete. "He told me his name is Tony," Nate reported as they carried the stretcher the hundred yards to the clinic. "He gave me a message for a Saint Charlotte who apparently teaches in that building."

"Lady Charlotte Winderfield," Blythe told him. "She established and supports the school. I expect he's one of her students."

Nate put aside his curiosity, and his elation at another opportunity to see his beloved's sister. He had a patient to treat, but in the morning, he'd convey the boy's message to Lady Charlotte.

The road conditions delayed the Duke of Winshire's arrival at his destination, forcing an overnight stop a mere two-thirds of the way through the journey. He and his men travelled with two extra mounts each, which would have meant a seven-hour journey without the rain, the thick mud, and the cold.

Even to be on time for his appointment, Winshire wasn't prepared to risk the horses, but nor did he want to leave a trail of reports about his travels. They stopped in whatever shelter they could find when the horses needed rest, and camped for the night before the sun set.

They rose early the next day and broke their fast as they rode, but still, it was nearing noon when the church spire that had been described to him first came into sight. Winshire gave the signal to halt, and called for the English-bred horse he'd brought for the last part of his errand. He did not expect to be seen at his destination, but he had been asked for discretion. The Turkmen horses he preferred were distinctive, and would mark him as part of the Winshire household even if no possible observer could identify him as the duke.

"I should be no more than two or three hours," he told those who had accompanied him. Their commander frowned, but did not reiterate his arguments for accompanying Winshire. Undoubtedly, he or one of his men would follow at a distance, but they all knew how to stay out of sight, so Winshire didn't care about that.

The farm track to which he'd been directed skirted the village and brought him to the meeting place fewer than ten minutes after he left his guard. As he dismounted, a man came out of the small outbuilding. Did he have the wrong place? Had her plan been discovered?

The man's words put him at ease. "I'll look to your horse, sir. You are to go straight inside." So. She had not come unaccompanied. *Of course not, and quite right, too.* Though this little lodge was on the fringes of the main estate, it was still isolated, and a likely target for those poor displaced souls, often former soldiers, who roamed the countryside looking for food, shelter, money or people from whom they could wrest such necessities.

Winshire looked around as he knocked on the door. The cottage had been kept in good repair, but nevertheless had an air of abandonment. He was trying to nail down what details indicated it was unloved in when the door opened. He turned to ask to be shown to his hostess, or allowed to wait for her inside until she could see him. There she stood, her warm smile the only welcome he needed.

He could feel his own smile growing in response. "Eleanor."

The Duchess of Haverford stepped back to give him space to enter. "James. Come in!"

He followed her across a small entrance hall to a cosy little parlour, where a fire burned in the hearth and a tray with a tea set waited on a small table between two chairs. Eleanor took the seat closest to the teapot and waved her hand to the other. "Be seated, dear friend. Would you care for tea?"

Tea is not what I hunger for. For ten years after Mahzad's death, he had thought himself beyond desire, but Eleanor brought it roaring back the first time he saw her on his return to England. Getting to know her again had only increased his longing; she was even lovelier, both within and without, than when they had first met long ago, before her father accepted the Duke of Haverford's suit for her hand, and rejected that of James, who was only the third son of the Duke of Winshire.

James was forced into exile and Eleanor was made to marry Haverford.

He kept his feelings to himself. If he told her his hopes, and if she shared them, he didn't trust himself to be alone with her like this without besmirching his honour and insulting hers.

Eleanor was a married woman and virtuous, even if her husband was a monster. Even if the old devil was rotting from within and locked away for his own good and to protect the duchy. James accepted the offered seat and the cup of tea; asked after the duchess's sons and wards and caught her up to date with his own family; exchanged comments on the war news and the state of the harvest.

"James," she said at last, "I proposed this meeting for a reason."

"To see me, I hope. Since Parliament went into recess and we both left London, I have missed our weekly visits to that little book-shop you frequent."

Eleanor smiled, and James fancied that he saw her heart in her eyes for a moment, and it leapt to match his. But her smile faded and her lashes veiled her eyes. "That, too, my dear friend. I have missed you, too. But there is another matter I need to bring to your attention."

She grimaced and gave her head a couple of impatient shakes. "It seems I am always muddying our time together with gossip and scandal. I am so sorry, James."

"One day, I hope we will be able to meet without subterfuge, and for no reason but our pleasure," James said. The last word was a mistake. He might be old, but at the word 'pleasure', his body was reminding him urgently that he was not yet dead.

Eleanor seemed unaffected, focused on whatever bad news she had to give him. "You are aware, I am sure, of the history of your niece Sarah's ward?"

"Her son?" James queried. He had assumed Eleanor knew. She was a confidante of his sister-in-law.

"Indeed. What you may not know—what I have just found out —is that Society is making that assumption and spreading the story."

James shook his head. "I guessed the gossips and busybodies would reach that conclusion, but without proof or confirmation, and with the family firmly behind her, the rumours will die."

"True, if that was all. But James, you may not know—Sarah may not know—that her little boy's father is back in England and, if my sources are accurate, seeking a bride."

James stiffened. "The coward has returned?"

"As to that," Eleanor said, "Grace always suspected that Sutton and Winshire had something to do with his disappearance, and it is being whispered that his father has recently bought him out of the navy, where he had worked his way up to being a surgeon."

"And your sources are associating Sarah and her child with this man?"

Eleanor shook her head. "Not yet. The two rumours are separate. But if the two of them meet, people may make connections. Especially if the child resembles his father." She shrugged, even that small elegant movement unusually casual for the duchess. "It is all very manageable, James, but you needed to know."

"I appreciate it, Eleanor." He sighed. "English Society is more of a snake pit than the court of the Shah of Shahs or that of the Ottoman Sultan Khan. Tell me, what is going on between my niece Charlotte and your son Aldridge?"

Eleanor's answer was hasty, but her eyes slid away from his. "Nothing. There can be nothing between Charlotte and Aldridge."

7

———

By the second week of the house party, Sarah had discounted all three of her possible suitors, and hadn't added anyone to her list. None of them improved on closer acquaintance. Or perhaps it was just that she couldn't move forward now that Nate had come back into her life. She had to hear him out, as her sister had urged her. Then, when he had told her whatever lies he'd dreamt up to explain his sudden disappearance just when she needed him most, she would be able to put him firmly back in the past, where he belonged.

Elias wasn't enjoying the party, either. He asked several times when they could go home, and his nursemaid reported the kind of subtle bullying that is hard for adults to counter because every edged remark, every shove or poke, could be explained away as innocent or accidental.

When Sarah received Charlotte's letter about a missing protégé, she was relieved. "Please make my apologies to Lady de Witt," Charlotte had written. Sarah looked for her hostess and explained that her sister Charlotte was dealing with a small family emergency. "I regret that I will need to return to London immediately," she added.

"In the morning, surely," Lady de Witt suggested. "You won't want to travel in the dark, and if you leave at daybreak tomorrow, you will still be back in London for lunch."

Having once entertained the thought of leaving the party early, Sarah couldn't bear to delay. Drew agreed with an alacrity that hinted he'd had his own difficulties with the other guests. They would stop at the inn that marked the halfway point, and be on their way again as soon after dawn as they could manage. Sarah, Drew, Elias, and their servants left Lady de Witt's manor within the hour, Drew riding escort while Sarah and Elias shared the first carriage and the servants took the second.

They rode in silence at first. Elias knelt on the seat so he could look out the window, but Sarah could tell he was thinking deeply. They were still a few miles from the inn when Elias spoke.

"Is what they said true, my lady?" he asked. "Am I a by-blow? What is a by-blow?"

Sarah couldn't think what to say. This was Nate's fault. If he hadn't burst back into her life, she would have left Elias in London, safe in his own schoolroom, surrounded by people who loved him.

"Mr Wilson said I was a nobleman's cuckoo," Elias added, quoting the man in charge of the workhouse to which Elias had been taken after his foster parents died. "What does that mean, my lady? I don't understand."

Sarah had known she would have to explain to Elias one day, but not yet. Not when the child was only six years old. Not when they were still so new to one another.

"Now, then, Master Elias," the nursemaid interrupted. "Don't thee be bothering Lady Sarah with thy questions. She's taken thee in and it is grateful thee should be, think on."

Elias's fallen face was enough to break Sarah out of her paralysis. "Thank you, Morris, but Master Elias is welcome to talk to me about anything that bothers him. Elias, darling, 'by-blow' is a very rude word. It means a child born to two people who made a mistake, but you are not your parents, Elias. You are not the mistake they made, and anyone who thinks otherwise is a fool. You are a dear and precious person, and I love you."

Elias accepted the hug that Sarah could not resist giving, his usual hesitancy a momentary thing before he returned the embrace. "I love you, too, Lady Sarah."

Sarah threw caution to the wind. The *ton* would think the worst anyway, and Uncle James and her sister would stand by her whatever other people said. "Would you… Do you think you might wish to call me 'Mama', darling?" Perhaps it was time to follow her first plan, and retire to the country under another name.

Elias drew back without letting her go, meeting Sarah's gaze. His eyes brimmed with tears. "May I?"

Sarah nodded, her own eyes overflowing. Elias burrowed in again, muffling his next question. But Sarah heard it well enough. "Who were my real mother and father, Mama? Do you know?"

A collapsing wall brought a flood of injuries into the clinic just as the sky began to lighten, and it was well after dawn before Nate had time to check again on the boy Tony. He was sleeping, but he was breathing easily and showed no sign of fever.

Nate went to take his leave of Blythe, who thanked him for all his hard work. "You hit a busy night, Beauclair, and you proved your worth. I hope you'll stick to it. We need doctors, and few are willing to give up their time to those who can't pay."

Nate decided the Winshire mansion—townhouse was too unpretentious a word—was not far out of his way on his drive home, so gave that address to the driver of the hire carriage he found a few doors from the clinic. No fashionable lady would be up at such a time, but he could leave a note to be given to her with her morning cup of chocolate, or whatever she ordered when she woke up.

But when the carriage stopped outside of the main doors to the mansion, several horses and riders waited in the street. He recognised Lady Charlotte by the steps, talking to—arguing with, by the looks of it—a fair-haired man. "Wait here for me," he told the driver. "I'll want to go to Fairview Square after this."

The three men with the horses were Winshire's fearsome foreign guard, who watched him as he strode towards the lady. Their faces were impassive, but he had no doubt that any untoward move on his part would be terminally unwise.

The man Lady Charlotte was talking to, though, put a hitch in his step—the Marquis of Aldridge, who was the son and heir of the Duke of Haverford. The marquis had been pointed out to him by Libby one evening, and she had favoured him with a brief summary of the aristocrat's career as a rake and his impending elevation to one of the highest titles in the land, given the approaching death of his father.

She had also speculated whether the feud between the Haverfords and the Winshires would continue for another generation. Given the warmth in Aldridge's eyes as he observed Lady Charlotte watching Nate approach, Nate rather thought he could answer that question.

"You are early, Lord Bentham," she greeted him. "My sister is still away."

"I came to see you this morning, my lady. Or at least to leave you a message. I expected to be told you were not available to visitors."

"I have been out early," Charlotte agreed, "and I fear that we must go out again directly. Aldridge, have you meet Bentham, Lechton's heir?"

Nate nodded at Aldridge, heir to heir, but spoke to Lady Charlotte. "I have a message from a boy named Tony."

Everyone stilled, even the retainers. "Tony? You have seen him?"

"I treated him. He will recover." Always start with the most reassuring news. "He fell and broke a leg. Bruised ribs. A few bangs and cuts. He is safe and in the Ashbury Clinic in Brightwell Lane just off Wintermount Street."

"Ruth's clinic?"

Nate didn't know who Ruth was, so ignored Lady Charlotte's interpolation. "He said to tell you he did not run. He was taken from the garden."

"There, Aldridge," Charlotte said to the marquis. "I told you.

Thank you, Lord Bentham. Yahzak, can we go now?"

"Is he awake, Bentham?" Aldridge asked, and when Nate shook his head, he said, "Breakfast first, now that we know he is safe, my lady. I am sure your men are hungry, and I know I am. Why don't you invite Bentham to join us? He can tell us how Tony came to be at the clinic."

"I will dispatch a man to stand guard," the man addressed as Yahzak suggested, and at his nod another leapt on one of their magnificent horses and cantered away down the street.

"Dismiss your carriage, Bentham," Lady Charlotte suggested. "We'll see that you get home."

Over a lavish breakfast, Lady Charlotte quizzed Nate about Tony's condition. It soon became clear that she didn't want to leave him at the clinic. "Not if he can be safely moved, Lord Bentham."

"The kidnapper will try again," the Marquis of Aldridge warned, and Lady Charlotte's foreign-looking guard captain agreed. "He is in danger, and so are all at the clinic. Lady Ruth would not be pleased."

"Who is Lady Ruth?" Nate wondered aloud.

"My cousin Ruth is Lady Ashbury, the founder of the clinic," Lady Charlotte explained. Blythe had been full of stories about the foreign-trained female doctor who headed the establishment, but he'd never mentioned a title. Nate pulled his attention back to Lady Charlotte, who was asking a question. "Can Tony be moved, Lord Bentham?"

"I would prefer not, but it can be done if you are serious about the danger."

For a few minutes, they discussed logistics, and soon Nate was committed to going back to the clinic and escorting Tony home, making sure the boy was settled before seeking his own pillow.

"You can leave us to fetch the boy," Aldridge told Lady Charlotte. "You should rest, my lady."

Nate wondered what was between Lady Charlotte and Aldridge. The Merry Marquis, Society called him. Libby had appeared more enthralled than scandalised by the relatively mild anecdotes she'd shared, but Nate assumed the reality was far more unfit for a lady's ears, and Lady Charlotte did not appear to him to be a woman who would ignore those darker truths.

Nonetheless, the pair of them bickered for the rest of the meal like old adversaries—or lovers. Aldridge insisted the lady would not be safe travelling to and from the clinic escorted only by Nate and three of the fearsome warriors. Lady Charlotte told him he was being ridiculous. Which was true, and had Nate wondering all the more about their relationship.

Aldridge continued to urge that she stay home. "You must be tired," he pointed out. "You have been up all night."

"We have all been up all night," she responded. "And you have had a more active night than I, Lord Aldridge, and started earlier."

Aldridge opened his mouth to respond, looked at Nate, and swallowed whatever he was going to say. After a moment, he changed tack. "I have a family interest in the boy," he argued.

Nate thought that was the leveller, but he was wrong. Lady Charlotte didn't answer for several minutes, and then she adopted the appeal to authority tactic. "Of course, as the boy's uncle or father or brother, you must meet with Tony and ask your questions, but you will hardly be able to do so while he is in great pain, or unconscious. It shall be up to Lord Bentham, as his physician, to decide when he is well enough for visitors."

The inn was pleasant, and the beds comfortable in the suite given over to Sarah, Elias, her maid, and his nurse. Nonetheless, Sarah had been awake for hours, thinking about Elias and his question. He had accepted her response—that she would tell him about his mother and father when he was older. The task would have been easier if Nathaniel Beauclair had stayed away, no more than an unhealing wound in her memory.

Where on earth had he been? And why? At least he is alive! She should be relieved, but all the grief she had buried over the past seven years had turned to anger that he'd deliberately left her. Or, if not chosen to leave her—and he said not—he had deliberately stayed away.

Every time she began to drift off, her mind began to replay memories of the summer she turned sixteen; the summer she spent falling in love with Nate. And she would jerk herself back to full wakefulness, forcing her thoughts into a different channel.

It was worse when her tiredness finally submerged her into a disturbed sleep, when she relived in dreams the loss of her beloved, the duke's attempt to marry her to one of her father's friends, the discovery of her pregnancy and all that followed.

It was not full light when Elias woke before his nurse and came looking for her, waking her from a horrifying replay of her second loss, the theft of her son, by shaping her face with a curious finger.

Her heart still pounding, Sarah cupped his hand and held it against her face. "Elias, darling."

"Good morning, Mama. Mama, why are you crying?"

Was she? Ah, yes. Tears were running down her cheeks. "I was having a bad dream, Elias. I am so glad you woke me."

She sat up, and invited Elias to sit beside her, taking his hands to help him up onto the bed. The nurse found them chatting when she stumbled through half an hour later, full of apologies to Sarah and scolds for Elias. "You know you are not to go to Lady Sarah unless she sends for you."

"Not at all, Morris." Sarah squeezed the hand she had around Elias's shoulders, hugging him to her. "Elias must not wander around Winshire House, or any other big mansion, without you or some other adult with him. But at home in Oxfordshire, where the house is much smaller, and at times like this, when we are both in the same suite, he can reach my bedchamber safely. He may come to his mama at any time, but here, he does not need someone to bring him."

She dropped a kiss on his hair. When he had first come to live with her, he had stiffened at every touch, flinched even, and withdrawn from caresses as quickly as he could. Now, six months later, he leaned into her trustingly. She had lost six years of his life. Before long, by all she'd heard, he would consider himself too old for physical expressions of affection. She would make the most of the remainder of his childhood.

It was full light outside now, with enough light creeping in to see that Sarah's maid was awake, sitting up on the pallet near the door. "It seems we will be ready for an early start," Sarah commented, smiling at her across the room.

"I shall get dressed and fetch your washing water, my lady."

"Thank you. And see if Lord Andrew's manservant is up, will you? Ask him to let Drew know we are awake and eager for our breakfast." Drew was generally up with the dawn, even when he had been out all night doing whatever it was he did. Somehow, she couldn't see him wasting his time gambling and whoring. Although he was no older than she and Charlotte, he seemed much more mature than the young cubs of the same age who were dragged reluctantly by their mothers to the Season's more respectable events.

Sure enough, he was awake, and had already secured a private parlour for their breakfast. Within an hour, they were on their way, a fresh team of horses eating up the miles between them and London.

They were home at Winshire House by mid-morning. Elias and his nanny disappeared up the stairs to the nursery. Sarah paused at the bottom of the steps to watch him eagerly leading the way.

"He has come a long way in the last six months," Drew observed.

She turned to him with a smile. "He is naturally a sunny-natured fellow, I think, Drew. That helps."

"You know," Drew said, "marriage is for a very long time, cousin. If you cannot find Elias a father who also suits you, he does have a number of uncles who will be proud to love him and support him."

Sarah swallowed a lump in her throat. "I appreciate that more than I can say."

Drew gave her a quick one-armed hug and turned to the butler to change the subject. "Has my father returned, Grosvenor?"

"No, my lord, and we have no word to expect him today."

Drew nodded. "Thank you." He put one foot on the first stair and then turned back to Sarah. "I'm going to change and then eat. Will you join me for a second breakfast, cousin?"

"For a cup of tea, at least. Is my sister up, Grosvenor?"

"Lady Charlotte has not yet returned from the Ashbury Clinic, my lady, though we expect her shortly." An infinitesimal relaxation in his stiff demeanour preceded an explanation that, for Grosvenor, was decidedly chatty. "The boy she had staying with her was kidnapped, escaped and was then injured. She has gone to fetch him. The, er, female persons she sent to us have been accommodated in the minor guest bedrooms."

Sarah exchanged a questioning glance with Drew. Female persons? But the butler had taken a step closer to the front door. "Ah! That may be them, now!"

8

In the end, Aldridge had accepted his dismissal and gone home, while Nate and Lady Charlotte took a Winshire barouche, with plenty of room for a stretcher, to the clinic. Half-a-dozen horsemen escorted them, which suggested to Nate the danger to Lady Charlotte was not just in Aldridge's imagination.

At the clinic, all was quiet, today not being a public clinic day. Nate introduced himself to the orderly who bustled out when the bell on the door jangled. "I am Dr Beauclair, a new volunteer here. I was on duty last night, with Dr Blythe, and I have returned to collect the patient we brought in, a boy called Tony. This lady is his employer."

The orderly squinted at Lady Charlotte, then stammered, "I don't know nuthin' about that, sir. Dr Blythe is asleep, sir. I'll just get the doctor on duty, shall I?"

He sidled off and returned a few minutes later with a doctor Nate had met on the day of his interview, and was therefore able to present to Lady Charlotte. Soon, they were being shown upstairs to the ward.

"I gave the boy some laudanum," the man explained. "Pain, you know."

Probably as well for, as gentle as Lady Charlotte's men were, being moved while conscious would have been hard on the lad. Still, another dose so soon after the last would not have been Nate's choice. He kept his opinions to himself and followed the stretcher out to the barouche.

It was a well-sprung carriage, and young Tony was deeply unconscious. The driver avoided deeply rutted streets and went slowly. Even so, the unavoidable bumps wrenched groans from the boy, and Nate was relieved when they finally turned into the court-yard of the Winshire mansion.

The front door opened while one of the men was handing Lady Charlotte from the barouche and Nate was untying the straps that secured the stretcher to the seats.

"Charlotte!" It was her. Sarah. She didn't notice him standing there, gaping. He bent to his task again while she flew to her sister and demanded to know what was happening. "Grosvenor said there was a kidnapping!"

Perhaps I can slip away without being noticed, as she did from the dinner party at Lord and Lady Hamner's. He was exhausted, ready to drop in his tracks. He needed to be alert and refreshed before he explained himself to her.

But he heard Lady Charlotte say his name, and turned to find Lady Sarah at the carriage's steps, looking up at him. All the words he wanted to say to her melted away as she stood within reach at last, and only the steely glint in her eye and the certainty that the Winshire warriors would gut him prevented him from reaching out and filling his empty arms with the love he had never forgotten.

"A kidnapping, yes," Charlotte answered Sarah. "Tony was taken from the garden, but he managed to escape. He was injured, though. We don't know how. Lord Bentham found him and treated him at Ruth's clinic." She nodded towards the barouche, and Sarah turned to see Nate.

"He's a doctor," Charlotte muttered. "Trained in Edinburgh."

Nate quirked one eyebrow. "Not quite. I was sent for before I graduated. Lady Sarah, good morning. I'm skilled enough to keep this boy safe while we move him to the room you have prepared for him." He gestured to the waiting footmen. "One on each pole, and when you're ready to lift, wait for my word. We must be as smooth and steady as we can, so we don't jolt him."

Good morning? That is it? He waltzed back into her life after seven years and managed to fit a 'good morning' in between his remarks to her sister and his instructions for the care of his patient?

For a moment, Sarah had thought he was going to embrace her. Not that she would have welcomed it. Of course not. She couldn't possibly forgive what he had done to her—to her and to Elias. Even if her body yearned for his.

Ridiculous. Of course, it does not. He was not the boy Sarah remembered in any way. Taller, broader, more confident and powerful, the easy charm modulated into a stern, commanding air. *What has happened to him? Where has he been?*

She would find out. He owed her the explanation he had promised her through Charlotte. And once she knew, she could put him behind her for once and for all, and resume her search for a husband.

But not today. Today, she was tired—from the travel, the disappointing house party, her anxiety over the way Elias was being treated. She had made up her mind to refuse Nate any request for an interview today when she realised that he was following the stretcher into the house without another word to her.

"Is something wrong?" Charlotte asked, coming to put an arm around her.

Sarah didn't answer, because Nate had stopped in the doorway and was looking back at her. The imperturbable mask was down, and he gazed at her with naked yearning. "He looks tired," she commented.

She hadn't really been talking to Charlotte, but her sister answered, "He worked a full night at the clinic, and has not yet been to bed. Are you going to let him tell you his story, Sarah?"

Nate had entered the house after the stretcher. Sarah and Charlotte mounted the steps, still arm in arm as Sarah thought about her answer and saw an opportunity to escape.

The stretcher party was partway up the main staircase. Sarah gave her sister a squeeze. "I'll leave you to see Tony settled, and then you should get some sleep yourself, and so should Lord Bentham. Tell him to wait upon me tomorrow at eleven. I am going up the family stairs to see if all is well in the nursery."

Charlotte yawned. "When you are free, you might ask Mrs Arbuckle where she has put my other guests. Two women from the Beast's pleasure house who helped Tony escape. Sarah, Uncle James's investigators have found out the Beast is Wharton. He has been building a new empire in the slums under his new name."

Stanley Wharton, who was then calling himself the Duke of Devil's Kitchen, had been behind many of the attacks on the Winderfields since Uncle James arrived back in England. Last year, he had kidnapped their cousin Ruth and the daughter of the Earl of Ashbury, who was now Ruth's husband. He'd broken out of prison and was believed to be in the West Indies with his sister, Ashbury's sister-in-law.

Charlotte said, "I've promised the women shelter until we can make a plan." She broke off for another huge yawn. "Perhaps you might tell them about Oxfordshire? And see what skills they have?"

Sarah smiled. "You are exhausted, darling. Leave your fallen women to me and the housekeeper, get your young man settled, and go to sleep."

After all, wild schoolboys were Charlotte's field of interest. Sarah was the one who had followed their aunt and mother into looking after women who had been seduced, abused, neglected and abandoned. Not that the village in Oxfordshire would be welcoming to women who had actually worked in a brothel. *But I know who will.*

After visiting the nursery to find Elias happily at work on his letters—he was rapidly making up the education he'd missed—she instructed the frowning housekeeper to take her to her sister's two guests.

The housekeeper, Mrs Arbuckle, made her disapproval of Charlotte's guests clear without openly criticising Charlotte. "I have put them on the third floor, in the guest wing, my lady."

"One of the rooms for visiting upper servants," Sarah noted.

"Not appropriate, I know, my lady, but I could not put them near my girls, could I? And we have no visitors to be offended at the moment." She continued to bustle through the house, her swift no-nonsense steps very different to the glide that ladies were taught from the moment they graduated from toddling.

"I will stay with you, of course," Mrs Arbuckle added.

"Not necessary, Mrs Arbuckle. You may send a maid with tea and cakes, but I will interview the two women on my own." The aristocratic tone, Sarah had found, worked with servants who had not known one from birth. Those who had seen her toddle in leading strings tended to ignore it.

Mrs Arbuckle, a new hire since Uncle James inherited the title, accepted her dismissal with no more reaction than tightly crimped lips, pointing to the door of the chamber allocated to the visitors, and retreated down the hall.

When Sarah knocked on the door, a cheerful voice called, "Come in, love. It's not locked!"

She stopped, just inside the room. Clothes were strewn across the bed, a sofa, one of the three chairs and the two chests against the wall. A large hip bath stood to one side of the fireplace, and a screen stood to the other side. Two pair of bare feet were visible under the screen.

"'Elp yerself to the barf water, love. We've finished," said the same person who had invited her to enter.

"I am not here for the bathwater," Sarah explained.

A head popped out one side of the screen.

"Eee, Bets, it's never a maid."

"I am Lady Sarah, Lady Charlotte's sister. I've come to talk to you about what you would like to do next."

Both women emerged. They wore skimpy chemises and nothing else. Furthermore, Sarah could see their figures and the dark shapes of their nipples and their nether hair through the thin material. Damp hair hung around their shoulders—in the case of the petite blonde, all the way to her derrière. Where hair had touched fabric, it was fully transparent.

The dark-haired one explained, "We was drying our hair, my lady. We thought we'd better hide when you knocked in case you was a footman come for the bathwater. That Mrs Arbuckle said we wasn't to make up to the servants, 'cause if we did, she'd put us out into the street whatever Lady Charlotte said."

"She won't," Sarah assured them, "but your courtesy in not placing temptation in the way of the footmen is appreciated. My sister asked me to see if I could help you to safety and a new life, if you want one." She waved to the piles of clothes. "Perhaps you could put on a robe, and we could sit and talk?"

The two women exchanged a glance and then obeyed, sitting together on a sofa opposite the chair Sarah had taken. The robes were gaudy garments in sateen—one with purple dragons and blue flowers printed on a scarlet background, the other a vivid pink with multicoloured flowers that never grew in nature. At least they covered the essentials, though they were short in length and open almost to the waist.

"As I said, my name is Lady Sarah Winderfield. And you are?"

"Elizabeth Cotton, my lady," said the brunette, who appeared to have appointed herself spokesperson. "But I'm mostly called Bets. And this is Sadie Fletcher." Her accent was almost gone, Sarah noticed. She might almost pass for a gentry woman, by her voice alone, when she made the effort to speak well.

"Sarah," the blonde corrected. "I've always been called Sadie, but my for real name is Sarah, if you don't think it impertinent, my lady."

"Cor. I never knew that," Bets told her friend.

Sadie shrugged. "Doesn't matter none. I just thought it was maybe a sign." She turned hopeful eyes on Sarah. "You and me having the same name, like." She flinched at her own words, as if expecting a blow.

"Perhaps it is," Sarah told her.

They were interrupted by another knock on the door. Sarah

called, "Enter," and a maid backed into the room with a tray of tea things.

"Thank you, Anne," Sarah said. "Just put it on the table here, and we'll serve ourselves."

She busied herself preparing a cup for each of them, with an internal smile at what the Earl of Colyton would think of her serving tea and cake to a pair of harlots. *Pompous prat.*

If she'd made a wager on which of them would return to the purpose of the meeting, she would have picked Bets, and she would have won.

"Excuse me for speaking out of turn, my lady, but how can a lady like you help the likes of us to"—she put on an exaggerated *ton* accent—"'safety and a new life'?"

Sarah put her cup on its saucer. "That is a fair question, Miss Cotton."

Bets turned a delighted face to her friend and whispered, "Miss Cotton."

Sarah ignored the interruption. "I am going to trust you with a secret." Not as much of a secret as it used to be. Since her uncle had become duke, she, her mother, and her Aunt Georgie had had his full support for their rescue work, and a duke's support protected them from the worst consequences of their actions. "I am one of a group of ladies who help gentlewomen escape from violent men."

"We ain't gentlewomen, my lady," Sadie pointed out. "I'm a foundling and Bets was a farmhand's daughter before she came to London."

Sarah nodded her acknowledgement. "Through my work, though, I've come into contact with others who help those who are not gentry. Have you heard of the Theodora Foundation?"

Both women shook their heads.

"It is a training school for women who have been selling sexual favours and who wish to leave that life. It offers a place to stay while they recover, and teaches new skills where needed. If a woman remains with the school for three months and is of good character during that time, the sponsors of the school will help her to find employment."

"Like...a sort of Magdalene Hospital, my lady?" Bets asked, cautiously.

"Most unlike," Sarah assured them. "The founders see little reason to punish those who have decided to turn over a new leaf. However, if you are not interested, my sister and I can help you get to a city beyond the Beast's reach, with enough money for a place to stay until you find another position within your current"—she paused, trying to find the right word—"trade."

"If I went to the Fedora, I could leave?" Sadie asked.

"The Theodora Foundation? Yes. At any time. The doors are never locked, and women come and go all the time. Though I warn you, if you left and went back to your former life, you would not be welcome back."

The two women had more questions, and Sarah answered as best she could. Bets was pleased to discover that the Foundation was in the country, some way from London. Sadie, who had seldom left London's slums and never the sprawling metropolis itself, was more apprehensive. In the end, they both decided to, as Bets put it, "Give it a go, 'cause we ain't getting any younger, and the way we're going we'll wind up dead."

"I'll send a message to the London agent of the Foundation. You will need to go for an interview. But I will speak for you and so will my sister. I am sure you will be accepted." A vicar of her acquaintance, Alex Basingstoke, ran the London end of the Foundation from his parish on the outskirts of Clerkenwell. Sarah had known his wife, Lady Freddie, all her life. Alex and Freddie had heard every story possible, but Sarah was sure they'd judge Bets and Sadie as sincere.

Sarah left the two women in a cheerful discussion about what sort of job they might want to learn skills for, and headed up to the suite she shared with her sister.

The Beast had brooded all day, ever since one of his minions had found a witness who had seen the boy Tony. The brat had been

treated for a broken leg at that free clinic the Ashbury bitch had
founded. The Winderfield cow, the one who taught at the free
school that stole children from their jobs, had picked Tony up and
taken him home.

Toffee-nosed aristocrats, interfering in the slums with their
schools and clinics and safe houses for runaway whores and others.
He would make them pay. He would make them all pay.

His sister argued against it. "Punish them by taking their money
at the tables, brother. By collecting their secrets in the chambers
upstairs and blackmailing them. You will have the army down on us
again."

Stupid female. Did he think he was foolish enough to show his
hand? He called for the lieutenant he trusted most.

"Scar, we are calling in debts and favours. Come onto my terri-
tory and take what is mine, will they? The clinic burns. The school,
too. Anything those interfering do-gooders support in the slums. I
want it all destroyed." He held up a finger. "Mind! All to be done
through others. I want the slums to rise up against them. Keep my
name out of it. We don't want to fight them head on."

Scar nodded, and hurried off to carry out his instructions.

The Beast sank back on his throne. "Not yet," he whispered.
"We will strike from the shadows until they are weak and we are
strong. We will take back what is ours and we will have our
revenge."

Before Sarah reached her rooms, a footman brought her a message
to say that the duke had returned home, and would like to see her.

He was in his study, standing before the fire with his hands
behind his back. He turned to greet her with a welcoming smile.
"Sarah. How went your holiday in the country?"

She was comfortable enough in his company to give a grimace
as her response and he showed his sympathy in his commiserating
smile.

"That bad, was it?"

"Elias was bullied, and my suitors proved themselves...unsuitable. Some of the company was pleasant enough, Uncle, but I am very tired of the pettiness and judgementalism of many who consider themselves the cream of Society."

His eyes flared with concern. "Was Elias hurt?"

"The bullying was verbal rather than physical. I fear that Elias has suffered worse in his short life. But he was pleased to leave, and I rather think Drew was, too."

The duke barked a short laugh. "He was. His opinion of Society marches with yours, and he found the company at the house party long on gossip and short on sense."

He sobered. "Speaking of your son and gossip, I have heard from someone I trust that people are questioning your relationship with Elias."

Sarah waved a dismissive hand. "They will pass on to some other topic soon enough. They can prove nothing."

"No one has suggested a candidate for Elias's father, but I am given to understand... Sarah, is the new Viscount Bentham the man?"

Sarah could only nod. How did Uncle James know? Most of those who knew the secret were dead. *Surely Mama and Aunt Georgie have betrayed me?* But her uncle was their brother. Would they have kept the secret if he asked the question? *What will he do now that he knows?*

"Drew tells me that Bentham was here when you arrived home this morning," His Grace commented.

Meaning what? Did her uncle think she had taken up again with the man who had betrayed her so cruelly? "He is a doctor, or so he says. He was attending the urchin to whom Charlotte is offering shelter."

The duke shook his head in bemusement. "So Drew says. Something about a kidnapping, a visit to a brothel, and an escape with two young women as souvenirs. What is Bentham to you now, my dear niece?"

It was a question without an answer—all the pain warring with the helpless longing he could still induce, despite their pasts, despite the multitude of ways in which they had both changed.

"Am I to welcome him to the family?" the duke asked, inexorable. She knew he cared for her, wanted to protect her, but her heart cried, *Leave me alone.*

"He wants to explain, he says," she blurted. "But what explanation can there be? I thought we were married! He told me the wedding was legal, that I was his wife, that he would make all right with my father." She blinked hard and stiffened her face against the tears. "And then he disappeared and my father told me that he'd lied; that he must have known the marriage was not legal since I did not have my father's consent to the match."

She sighed, remembering that terrible time. "I was ruined and he was gone. They told me he took money to leave, but I didn't believe them. I thought he must be dead. I was so sure that if he lived, he would come back to me." The tears spilled down her cheeks despite her best efforts. "But he is alive, so I was wrong. He did not come home!"

The duke pursed his lips, then took her by the elbow and led her to a chair, handing her a crisp white handkerchief. "I think I need to hear the whole story, dear Sarah. Sit, and explain. When did Bentham wed you, and where? This was, I take it, before Elias was born?" He sat in the chair beside hers, clasping her hand, his eyes still as kind and as calm as ever.

"It was before Elias was conceived," Sarah insisted, flushing, because that had been more by good luck than good management. She took a deep breath to compose herself. Uncle James had not berated her for the story so far; had continued to call her 'dear'.

"We were at Applemorn Hall in Somerset. Charlotte and I had mumps, and Charlotte was very sick. Mama decided that we should convalesce at Applemorn, where Bath was close enough that Charlotte could take the waters."

Her voice softened and she smiled a little. "Nate and I had seen one another on earlier visits. Mama liked Applemorn in summer, and we often stayed there. But he and I did not really meet until that summer."

"How old were you, Sarah?"

"Fifteen, when we arrived. I had my sixteenth birthday while we were waiting... Well, I shall get to that."

"And Bentham?"

"Nate, he was then. Nathaniel Beauclair, the vicar's son. I knew he had an earl somewhere on the family tree, but his father was not in line for the title. He was—is, I suppose—a year older than me."

"So, you came to convalesce and you and Charlotte renewed your acquaintance with the vicar's son," he prompted.

"Me, mostly. Charlotte had been very sick, as I said, and she spent a lot of time sleeping. I met Nate in the woods, and we liked each other. We were both lonely. Nate was expected to act as his father's secretary and messenger boy, carrying out many of the obligations of the parish. I visited the sick with him, and helped set up the church for services. At first, it was something to do, and then... We fell in love, Uncle James. At least, I fell in love, and Nate said he did."

She sat looking into the fire, remembering the heady feeling, the long afternoons discussing a golden future, stolen kisses—no—kisses freely given and received. The duke said nothing, waiting for her to continue.

"He took French leave of his father to go to Brighton, where my father was, to ask for permission to court me."

"Bold," the duke commented.

Sarah nodded her agreement. "He had a small inheritance from his maternal grandfather, and he thought he could find work as a secretary."

She had warned him that the duke her grandfather had more grandiose plans for her. He had kissed her and assured her of success. "Lord Sutton is your father, my Sarah. He and the duke will want your happiness, surely? God meant us for one another, I am certain of it."

Sarah had been right. "My father would not listen. A commoner. The son of a cadet branch of a noble family with nothing to recommend him as a suitor. That's what Father said when he had him ejected from the house. By the time the mail coach delivered Nate back to the vicarage, Father's messenger had already been there, and Nate was exiled to a relative in Oxfordshire, forbidden ever to come near me again."

He had climbed out the window and escaped up to the manor to tell her the whole. In whispers. "My father told him that he was negotiating with three men as potential husbands for me and Charlotte: the Duke of Richport, the Earl of Selby, and Viscount Rutledge. And if none of them were interested, my father had several friends who might want a young wife." She shuddered.

Even Sarah, then a sheltered schoolgirl, had been warned about those three men, and Nate knew more. He was frightened for her, he said. They had agreed that he must obey his father for the moment, but that they would write to one another and discuss what they must do. That night, afraid she would never see him again, Sarah had enticed him to stay the night in her bed and they had made love for the first time.

The next day, Nate was escorted to Brighton and put on the mail coach to Cheltenham and then to Lechford in Oxfordshire. The day after, the twins' older brother, Viscount Elfingham, arrived at Applemorn. "Father sent Elfingham to guard me, and to make sure that Mr Beauclair—he is the Earl of Lechton now, Uncle James, but then he was well down the line of succession—to make sure that Mr Beauclair had sent Nate away as commanded."

"I take it that Elfingham did not prove an effective chaperone," Uncle James commented.

"Elfingham spent several days telling me that Father was arranging a splendid match for me and I was not to ruin it by throwing myself away on a penniless vicar's son. For the rest of week, he grumbled about being stuck in the country with nothing to do but watch two little girls read books and make daisy chains." She managed a watery chuckle. "And you may be sure, Uncle, that we were careful to be as childish and as boring as we could. Until he started an affair with our governess and forgot all about us."

Poor Bella. Sarah and Charlotte tried to tell her not to believe Elfingham's promises, but Bella was starry-eyed at captivating a duke's heir and wouldn't listen.

"I take it your swain came up with a plan."

Sarah frowned. Nate had been so certain, so convincing. "He and his cousin. He said if we married, our fathers would have to accept it. He arranged it all. All I had to do was be ready to travel to Oxfordshire when he came for me."

She had wanted to believe him. "He said he'd had the banns read. He said as long as no one objected, our marriage would be legal."

"And he came to fetch you. Surely Elfingham noticed?"

"Charlotte feigned illness, and was seen around the house wearing a blonde wig. Elfingham never bothered to talk to us, or do more than poke his head around the door to check that I was still there. It worked well enough. We only needed a few days start."

They were three days on the road in the hired carriage, hurrying from post to post by day, sleeping in one another's arms by night. Just sleeping, because it was the time of her monthly indisposition. How gentle, how loving, how controlled Nate had been. Even the last night before their wedding, when she was well again.

Then they arrived, and within a few hours, they were married, or so she thought. Nate's cousin had been an unworldly man convinced he was helping in a righteous cause. He was curate in the tiny village of Lesser Lechford. He performed the ceremony and put a cottage at the newlyweds' disposal. She and Nate discovered the joys of marital intimacy, and they did not stir out of doors for three days.

"We were married, and spent several days together, but then one morning, Nate said we needed fresh milk and bread, and he left me to walk into the village. He never came back. My father arrived, instead, and told me that I had never been married, and that Nate had taken ten thousand pounds to leave England."

Uncle James knew the rest. The pressure to marry, which ended when she discovered she was with child. Hiding the pregnancy and birth from Society. And all the long years between when she had barely avoided her father's and grandfather's matrimonial plans for her.

"Between your father and Bentham, which would you have trusted to tell the truth?" the duke asked.

He knew the answer, of course. Her father would say anything that suited his purposes, with no regard for the truth. She had held on for years to the hope that they had driven Nate away, and he would return when she was twenty-one and free to make her own choices. All the time, she feared he must be dead.

"Nate left, Uncle James. He didn't write. He didn't come back. Not even two years ago, when I turned twenty-one and no-one could have stopped me from marrying him again."

"Three things give me pause, dear niece. One is that, even seven years ago, my brother would have had trouble laying hands on such a sum. The duchy was living on borrowed money and getting further and further into debt for fifteen years before I came back to England. The second is that your father and grandfather made no real attempt to force you into marriage. Not you, and not Charlotte, either. Many men would accept a duke's granddaughter without a dowry; some would pay for the privilege, and not mind a past scandal, either."

Sarah shook her head, slowly, not sure what to make of it all. Certainly, Father had talked about arranging a match for them both. Grandfather, too, after Father died. But they never mentioned specifics; never actually came up with candidates. She knew why they treated Charlotte so carefully, but why did they let her get away with refusing them?

Uncle James added, "My third reason to be open to believing your young man is that my father and brother did something similar to me. I planned a marriage that the duke forbade, so they had me beaten and thrown on a ship for the Levant, where I was left with a letter telling me that my beloved had married someone else, and I was forbidden to step foot in these united kingdoms until further notice."

Sarah tried to ignore the lifting of her heart. "I don't know what to think, Uncle James."

"I think you need to give your young man the opportunity to explain himself, Sarah. And then we will talk again."

9

N ate was awakened in the middle of the afternoon by the sound of his father, shouting. "Get him up now and tell him Lord Lechton demands he come out here immediately." Nate's manservant's voice was softer—Nate couldn't hear his words, but assumed he was trying to put the old man off. Nate had instructed he was not to be awakened until it was time to dress for whatever Libby had in store for them tonight.

"It's fine, Jackson," he called. "I am awake. Bring my father a glass of brandy and come and help me dress."

"Be quick about it," Lechton shouted. "You have some explaining to do, Bentham."

Lechton was pacing back and forth across Nate's small sitting room when Nate emerged from his bedchamber less than five minutes later. "You need a shave, and you shouldn't appear before me half dressed," Lechton greeted him.

Nate finished buttoning his waistcoat. "You said to be quick," he reminded the man.

"Now, you obey me?" Lechton stamped one foot, looking for all the world like a choleric bull. "I told you to give up this doctoring rubbish. I told you to stay away from the Winderfield woman. I am your father! You owe me your obedience!"

As far as Nate was concerned, Lechton had ceased to have any rights as his father when he betrayed Nate to the Earl of Sutton and signed the papers to have Nate consigned to the navy.

Lechton took Nate's silence in bad part. "You cannot deny it. I saw you leaving that clinic place. I asked questions. You had spent the night there pretending to be a doctor, and you were on your way to the Winderfield mansion with a patient."

The old man was spying on him now? Presumably he had been visiting one of the houses of entertainment in the area. Nate should ask him the name of the brothel he'd been at. No. No point in getting into a shouting match to edify all the neighbours. "I will continue to serve at the Ashbury Clinic, my lord, and I intend to reconcile with my wife as soon as possible."

Lechton gaped, then gobbled like a turkey, unable to form intelligible words in his anger.

"Sit down, my lord," Nate advised, "and take a sip of brandy."

His father plopped into a seat. Just as well only a small portion remained in the glass, or he would be wearing it. Nate picked up the bottle and poured a little more, and Lechton took a gulp.

"I'll bring you to heel," he threatened. "I will cut you off without a penny. No more allowance."

"The threat would be more effective if you had ever paid me an allowance," Nate drawled, which prompted another gobble and another gulp.

"The marriage was invalid. You were both minors," Lechton insisted, next.

Nate shrugged. "The banns were read. Neither guardian objected. We were legally wed." He wasn't nearly as confident of that as he tried to sound. His seventeen-year-old self had read a case in the papers about a young couple who settled far from where they were known and married that way. The courts had held that the banns had been read in public, allowing the guardians to object, and since they had not done so (even though the reason for their forbearance was that they weren't there and weren't told), the marriage was legal.

Nate had discussed a similar plan with his cousin, doing his best to reproduce the conditions in the newspaper account. Cousin Arthur agreed it sounded reasonable. He knew even more than Nate about the Earl of Sutton's proposed suitors for his daughters, and was prepared to do anything he could to help keep Lady Sarah from such a cruel fate.

But neither of the people in the article had a wealthy duke for a grandfather. Winshire might have been able to have the marriage annulled. No matter. If they were no longer married, they could always wed again. If Sarah would agree. If affection between them was reignited as easily as the physical attraction.

"I have her father's word. The marriage was invalid," Lechton repeated. His voice turned pleading. "Forget Sarah Winderfield. There are plenty of younger, prettier girls on the market."

"Lady Bentham," Nate corrected. "She has been my wife these seven years, even though you conspired with her father and brother to part us." Which was unfair. Lechton had been Winshire's lackey, not his ally. He was a weak and foolish old man, but not a monster.

Lechton drew himself up to his full height, still some inches short of Nate's near six feet. "You are not married. But I shall see about rectifying that immediately. I can see you have no intention of seeking a bride, so I shall arrange a marriage for you, and you can put all this nonsense behind you."

"Don't do it, my lord. I shall not sign any papers. I shall not agree to any marriage you arrange."

"You will if you want to see my wife and your sisters ever again." Lechton sneered, clearly thinking he had a winning hand.

Nate heaved a sigh. "I would regret such a split, and I hope you will not carry out a threat that would hurt them as much as me. But if that is the price I must pay to keep my promises, then so be it. My man will show you out, my lord."

Lechton managed a few more indignant splutters and some other toothless threats before he finally left. The Ashbury Clinic was sponsored by a ducal family, and wouldn't dismiss him as a result of the bullying of an earl with limited social connections. And the new Duke of Winshire, by what Nate had heard, was a very different man to his predecessor. One, furthermore, who allowed his own daughter to be a doctor.

Lechton was unlikely to get a hearing from the duke, and what would he say if he did? Nate was no longer the near penniless son of a humble vicar. He had been adding to his investments from his prize money for many years, and could well afford a wife. And the heir of an earl might aspire to the hand of a duke's daughter, even if he hadn't already married her years ago.

Really, Lechton, you are being ridiculous. Nate knew quite well what bee Lechton had in his bonnet. He was convinced a girl fresh out of the schoolroom was more likely to give him grandsons. As if a woman of three and twenty was past childbearing!

Nate sent his manservant out to buy them both something to eat, and sat down to write a letter to his father's cousin, the one who had helped him arrange his wedding. Not that he expected a reply. Previous letters had gone unanswered. He'd have to find someone to make enquiries, but meanwhile it couldn't hurt to write again—perhaps someone had been intercepting his letters to Arthur, as they must have done with those to Sarah.

The letter done and addressed, ready to be sent as soon as his manservant had time, he leant back in his chair to daydream about Sarah having his child.

Sarah stayed in her rooms when Nate came in the late afternoon to check on the boy Tony. Charlotte could attend the medical examination. Sarah was determined not to see Nate before the next day, as promised. Which meant a disturbed night, full of restless wondering, with steadily more unlikely scenarios floating in and out of her imagination and even more preposterous dreams when she managed to drift into a few minutes' sleep.

As a result, she slept in, then ate her breakfast with her sister in their private sitting room. By ten minutes before the hour of her meeting with Nate, she was downstairs. She had chosen to wait, with Charlotte for company and as chaperone, in one of the reception rooms near the front door, the better to keep this meeting on a formal basis.

This part of the house was strangely quiet. Apart from a footman in the entrance hall, she and Charlotte seemed to be alone, and Charlotte was lost in her own thoughts. Given all her sister had had to say about the Marquis of Aldridge last night—some praise and quite a bit of criticism—Sarah was guessing the man was still very much on Charlotte's mind.

Sarah's thoughts wouldn't settle. What could Nate—Lord Bentham—possibly have to say in his defence? Eleven o'clock came and went, with no Lord Bentham. He had let her down again. "He isn't coming," she said to Charlotte, after half an hour, then a commotion at the front door had her rising to her feet.

The door opened, and she braced herself to see him, but it was Drew who entered the room, and behind him she could see the entrance hall full of footmen and guards.

"What happened?" Charlotte asked. A good question. Drew, and the men behind him, looked as if they had been in a fight, or rolling in the mud, or... the reek of smoke gave her a clue... fighting a fire.

Sarah put her conclusion into words. "Where was the fire?"

"The Ashbury Clinic," Drew replied. "Sarah, Bentham sends his apologies. He is helping Ruth and the resident doctor to settle the patients they had to move to the Ashbury townhouse, and is then going home to change and wash."

"Was anyone hurt?" Charlotte asked.

Drew shook his head. "A few mild burns, some scratches. We got everyone out ahead of the fire. Put the fire out, too, though there's extensive damage, especially in the ward upstairs. We still have a building, though." He chuckled. "Aldridge caught some embers with his hair, and says his valet is probably going to resign."

Charlotte paled. "But not...Just his hair, Drew? He is not otherwise hurt?"

Drew shrugged. "Nothing serious."

"What were they all doing there?" Charlotte wondered. "Bentham and Ruth, I can understand, I suppose, though it seems an astonishing coincidence that they were available just when a fire started. But Aldridge?"

Drew shrugged. "Ruth was visiting, of course, as she does several times a week when she is in town. Just as well, too, for her guard were with her, and thought to send someone here for help. Ruth sent for Val, and Aldridge happened to be with him. Bentham turned up about the same time as I did. To check on a patient, he said."

Val was the Earl of Ashbury, Ruth's husband.

"I'm going to wash and change, cousins, if you will excuse me. There is more to the message from Bentham, Sarah. He apologises for missing his appointment. He says he will be here as soon as he can, and if you are not available this afternoon, he asks for a dance at the Farmington Ball this evening."

"I have a meeting with the Theodora Foundation," Sarah said. She checked the room's clock. "And will need to leave here in an hour or so. I will send him a message."

Drew rubbed a hand through his hair, looked at his hand, and shook his head. "My apologies, ladies, for coming to you in my dirt." He bowed himself out, then put his head back around the door. "Take a double guard, Sarah. We think the clinic fire was arson."

"My school!" Charlotte protested. "Excuse me, Sarah. I need to see if we can set a guard."

10

omeone had attempted to torch the school, Charlotte told Sarah in the carriage that evening, but several of the resident boys caught the arsonist at it, and put out the fire before it could take hold. "I suspect they were skipping classes to smoke in the alley," she said. "I would have asked, but I didn't want to tempt them to lie."

"So, who was it?" Sarah asked.

"That's the bad news. They called the runners and they took him away. I sent one of our men to question him, and he was gone. A 'gentleman' came and vouched for him."

"Bribes," Sarah assumed.

"Probably. Yahzak says he will find out. And, he will find the 'gentleman'. He has gone to talk to David Wakefield, Aldridge's brother."

"I spoke to Mrs Wakefield this afternoon," Sarah commented. "You know the Theodora Foundation has safe houses in the slums? Alex Basingstoke tells me that three of them have been attacked. And Mrs Wakefield has heard of more, including two other ragged schools. That's why I was late. We went to see the magistrates of all three London districts to warn them that someone is attacking charities that work with slum children and prostitutes."

Charlotte asked the obvious question. "Is this revenge for taking Tony and the women out of the brothel?"

Sarah shook her head. "Perhaps. But surely the Beast knows that he cannot get away with attacking institutions supported by gentry and the nobility? Can Tony help us put the Beast in jail?"

Charlotte shook her head. "He's a boy and an orphan from the slums. Even if we put him in front of a judge, the Beast is likely to claim he offered the boy a job. After all, Aldridge didn't actually see him in the room where he was imprisoned. Aldridge spent an hour with Tony this afternoon, by the way. They were trying to work out how they are related, though they're certain there is a connection."

"Is he Aldridge's son, do you think?" Sarah asked.

"Aldridge says not. He was in Scotland at the relevant times, and Tony says his mother lived in London." Charlotte examined her gloved fingers. "Aldridge takes his family responsibilities very seriously."

Whatever Aldridge had been like as a younger man, Sarah thought he now took all his responsibilities very seriously. The stories whispered among the ladies and joked over by the gentlemen were years old, though few people appeared to acknowledge any change.

The carriage had finally inched its way to the head of the line, and the footman opened the door for the sisters to descend. They expected Drew to be waiting, as he'd said he would meet them at the ball, but instead, Aldridge hovered on the steps and gestured to the footman to step aside so he could hand the ladies down.

The sisters couldn't help a quick gasp as he lifted his hat in greeting. His hair had been cropped close to his head, and on one side the skin showed pink and raw. Aldridge ignored the reaction with his usual insouciance. "Lord Andrew has been delayed, my ladies, but my mother is waiting to give you countenance this evening."

Charlotte looked about to argue that they were old enough to be able to attend a ball without a chaperone or a male family member, but Sarah nudged her. The throng working their way into the house did not need to be edified by watching Charlotte and Aldridge bicker.

Aldridge was known for his calm response in every situation. Sarah had only ever seen him become heated in discussion with two people: his half-sister Jessica and her sister Charlotte. And, whatever Charlotte might think, Sarah didn't think his feelings towards Charlotte were brotherly.

Speaking of Jessica, she was with the duchess, waiting in the mansion's entrance hall. She slipped her hand into Sarah's arm to ask after Elias. "I followed your example and used 'family matters' as an excuse to leave early. Aunt Eleanor is trying hard not to say 'I told you so'. She assured me that I would not enjoy a house party without either her or Aldridge to ensure people treated me with respect."

"Was it awful, Jess?"

Jessica shrugged. "They were not rude to my face, precisely. But they did use your poor little ward as an excuse to bait me. You know the sort of thing—talking about how the base-born should not be allowed to mix with decent people, and then apologising and looking flustered. Lord Colyton was kind, and Lord Hythe, of course. But most of them were horrid."

They had to break off to greet Lord and Lady Framington, their hosts. Sarah watched. The pair were as polite and friendly to Jessica as to her and her twin, but perhaps they couldn't do otherwise under the duchess's sharp eyes.

"I am sorry you had a terrible time," she murmured as they moved on up the stairs.

Jessica grinned. "I gave as good as I got. I pontificated about hypocrites and whited sepulchres, but very politely and without pointing any fingers. Silly people. We don't need them, do we, Sarah? Oh, look! Felicity is here! Aunt Eleanor, may I go and talk to Lady Felicity?"

The Framingtons must have been economising on candles, for only every second one was lit in the widely spaced chandeliers. This made the room too dimly lit and, even this early in the evening, too full of people to be able to pick identities at a distance, but their friend Lady Felicity Belvoir was chatting with friends in the nearest corner of the room, not twenty feet away.

"We'll all go," Charlotte suggested.

"I will make for the matron's corner," the duchess agreed. "Jessica..."

"I know, Aunt Eleanor. Stay with my friends, and if I am separated, perhaps to dance, have my escort bring me to you." Jessica managed to recite the litany without sighing and the duchess smiled.

"I know it annoys you, my dear, but a young lady needs to be careful."

The corner just to the left of the main entrance was, Sarah decided, as they exchanged greetings with their friend, an excellent place for Nate to find her. With that in mind, she had only half her attention on the conversation, the rest cataloguing the guests as they poured into the already crowded room, or trooped out on their way to some other entertainment.

More of the first than the second, so by the time the Earl and Countess of Lechton came in through the door, Nate a few feet behind them, the room had gone from 'crowded' to 'a crush' to 'a sad crush', and all four ladies had surrendered their dance cards several times to would-be partners.

Nate looked around, saw Sarah, and came straight to her. "Good evening, my lady." He remembered his manners and greeted Charlotte, who introduced him to Felicity and Jessica, but he delighted Sarah by being too flustered for more than a bow and a polite greeting, turning immediately to her to ask, "Did you get my message, my lady?"

"I did. I am sorry I had another errand this afternoon. You were not hurt in the fire, I hope?"

Then Felicity had to know what she was talking about, Jessica had to describe her shock at her brother's scorching, and Nate downplayed the event while casting glances sideways at Sarah. He was clearly wondering how to extricate himself from the conversation so he could talk to her.

She was about to ask him to escort her for a walk around the

room when Lord Farmington called for attention and announced
that the dancing was about to begin, and her first partner emerged
out of the hordes to claim her.

"I have you down for the supper dance, my lord," she told Nate
in an aside. "I will be waiting for you in the far corner—the one on
the right at the other end of the ballroom."

Nate gazed after her as she left. She could feel the weight of his
eyes, not just then, but throughout the next two hours, as she
accomplished three more sets with different partners, all the time
thinking about what Nate might have to tell her to justify his long
absence.

She had promised Uncle James she would listen. Indeed, she
would have done so without any such promise. Elias needed a father,
and here he was. And, apparently, her stupid heart didn't care about
his abandonment, and her even more foolish body was convinced it
belonged to him. She could feel herself melt when he was near, and
she'd never done that for anyone else.

If he had even a ghost of an excuse, she would have to get to
know him again. Not more than that. She didn't trust him, and she
wasn't sure he could mend that. She wouldn't marry without trust,
but she would give him a hearing.

The supper dance was a good choice. The first in the set was a line
dance. If he chose a group with a long line, particularly if he posi-
tioned them well, they could spend a fair part of the time standing
out, waiting for their turn in the patterns. The second was a waltz.
He realised his hopes were setting him up for disappointment, but
she had already softened to him. If she softened more after hearing
what he had to say, he would be able to hold her in his arms again,
even if it was on a dance floor, surrounded by half of the Polite
World.

Lady Framington introduced him to a young lady as a suitable
partner, so he took her out onto the floor. Then his father had one
of his insipid maidens to present him to, a Miss Tremaway,

daughter of a viscount. He escaped both her father and his by asking her for a dance, as well.

The next set was the one before the supper dance. He managed to avoid both his hostess and his father, prowling the end of the room where he was to meet Sarah. She was out on the floor, he noted, but Drew was in the corner where she'd told him to meet her, talking to a man who must be the Duke of Winshire. Yes, and the duke was sitting with the Duchess of Haverford, wife of his sworn enemy. He would have to ask Libby more about the relationship between the families.

Nothing, though, could long take his attention from Sarah, and he started for the corner when the musicians brought the current dance to a swirling end. He reached it before her, and Drew greeted him cheerfully. "Bentham! Have you seen Aldridge this evening?"

"Quite a haircut," Nate agreed. The hair had been singed away on one side, though the burns where it had caught fire were minor. They'd put the flames out quickly, and his clothes had protected his shoulder and arm, though the coat was a loss. Nate had smothered his head with salve, and the man would be fine, but he had presented an odd appearance, with hair long enough to touch his collar on one side and nothing on the other.

Since then, he'd had the whole head all but shaved. Anyone else might have stayed at home, but Aldridge ignored any change in his appearance as if it didn't exist. Except, perhaps, there was method in it.

Nate was familiar with the signs. The marquis had been pursuing Lady Charlotte, and she wanted nothing to do with him. But tonight, she was dancing with him. The action was unusual enough to have the ballroom buzzing.

Nate silently wished him luck, and tried to focus his attention as Drew presented him to the Duchess of Haverford and then to the Duke of Winshire. The older people exchanged a glance full of speculation. "You have a previous acquaintance with my niece," the duke said.

I am her husband, Nate wanted to shout, but he wouldn't make the claim until Sarah gave him leave. And until he was certain that the marriage stood, he supposed. In his heart, though, he was and always would be Sarah's whether their union had been legal or not; whether it had been annulled or not; whether she would let him love her again or not.

There she was. Yes, and Charlotte with Aldridge, who sent him a smile from one sufferer to another.

Nate endured a few more pleasantries, and at last offered Sarah his arm. "Let us skip the dance and find somewhere quiet to talk," Sarah said.

Nate looked at the doors to the terrace, tightly shut against the rain.

Sarah shook her head. "Not outside, and we can only talk at a shout in the ballroom, but the supper room should be quiet at the moment."

She guided him down the length of the room, across to the far wall, and through double doors in the corner, giving a sigh of relief as they stepped out of the noise and the heat.

It was another massive room, with tables set up at the far end. Near them, a dozen or more people already occupied some of the arranged groups of sofas and chairs, conversing or just resting from the activity in the next room.

Sarah led him to chairs a short distance from everyone else. "We can talk in private, without risk to your reputation and mine," she explained.

Again, Nate wanted to protest. His soul proclaimed he was her husband, and being private with her was no scandal, but rather the very definition of heaven! Not yet. First, he had an explanation to make, if he could only find the words to start.

"You left, Nate," Sarah said, when he remained silent. The desolation in her tone had his story tumbling from his lips, his fear of saying the wrong thing submerged by his desperate need to save her pain.

"I was abducted. You know the corner where our lane branched off from the road to the village? They were waiting in the trees. They jumped me as I passed. Three great brutes and your brother Elfingham. He stood back to see that I was thoroughly beaten." He hadn't meant to tell her the details, but perhaps it was for the best.

Sarah put a gentle hand on his arm. "They beat you? Oh, Nate."

He thrilled to her touch, every nerve under her hand suddenly at high alert. For a moment, he lost track of his story, but then he continued, "I tried to tell Elfingham that we were married; that you were my wife. He said it wasn't true, and if it was, the marriage would be annulled. I was being sent on a long sea voyage, and your father had arranged a marriage for you. I think your father was there too. I remember someone saying you'd be married within the month. They kept punching me and kicking me, and I must have passed out."

She slid her hand down to his and squeezed it, nibbling at her upper lip, her eyes brimming with tears. "Father came to our cottage. He told me that you had lied about our marriage, that you had taken money to leave me. I didn't believe him, Nate. But weeks passed and then months, and you didn't return."

"I couldn't. I woke up a week later, far out at sea." No need to mention the occasional surfacing into pain and nausea during the trip to the coast and the early part of the voyage. "When I demanded to speak to the captain, explained I had to get back to my wife, they laughed. My father had signed me over to the navy. I was enrolled for ten years as a common seaman, and I would not be allowed off the ship for any reason for at least the duration of the war. Much use I was going to be, he said." Even if he hadn't had several broken ribs, a broken arm, and who knew what internal injuries, he was a total landlubber.

"But you got away. For here you are," Sarah pointed out, "and, if gossip is true, you went to Edinburgh before the peace was signed."

The power of the *ton's* vast whispering chamber. "The ship's surgeon, Lieutenant Macintosh, wasn't that bad a sort. He took me on as a loblolly boy—a sort of assistant—as soon as I was well enough to be of use. When he found I knew a bit about rough first aid, he kept me on, and trained me as a ship's surgeon. By the time we'd been two years away, I no longer did much crew work. And after three years, Macintosh said I was ready to move to another ship in the fleet as their surgeon, and they made me a ship's surgeon, acting."

That still left four years, but he wanted to know about Sarah. And he wanted to keep her thinking hard enough that she didn't notice she still held his hand. "He didn't make you marry? Your father?"

She shook her head. "I was—ill, after you left."

Nate heard the hesitation. Had they beaten her, too? He looked over his shoulder to make sure the other occupants of the room could not see, and took her other hand in his free one. "I hate to think of you sick and in pain, and me not there to help."

"When I was well enough, my father and my grandfather tried to browbeat me into marriage to one of my father's friends, but Mama and Aunt Georgie stood up for me. I think, too, that by then they had spent my dowry, and I was harder to get rid of than they expected. And then Elfingham died and we were all in mourning." She shrugged. "I just kept saying 'no', whomever they suggested."

"You were very brave," Nate told her.

"Why didn't you write?" she asked. Then, looking up at him through her lashes, she made it a question. "Did you write?"

"To my cousin. I begged my cousin to find out how you were and to let me know. I even wrote to my father when I didn't hear from Arthur. Neither of them ever wrote back. I wrote directly to you, too, though I thought it would be useless. I assumed your father would keep any letters from you., but I still I posted letters whenever we were in port. I never got a reply."

"He isn't in Lesser Lechford. I rode over three years ago, after Mama and Charlotte and I retired to the dower house at Swinwood Hall. They told me he was accused of embezzling funds and corrupting minors. The bishop removed him from his post and nobody knew where he went. Nate, Grandfather must have done that to him, as revenge. Your poor cousin!"

Nate frowned. No wonder the man had never answered. He never received the letters. Then Nate had another thought. "I left our marriage lines with him for safekeeping. I wrote again last night to ask him to send them to me. I will find him, Sarah."

"We are really married?" Sarah asked, leaning towards him, and he smiled and nodded.

Just then, someone called Nate's title. "Bentham!" Lord Hythe, whom he'd met at White's and again at various entertainments, crossed the room from the doorway. "Your father was looking for you, Bentham. He wants you in the ballroom for some kind of an announcement."

Even as he spoke, they heard the music draw to a close, and someone began calling for silence. As the post-dance chatter died away, the last half of a sentence came to them, loud and clear: "...ado, I'll hand the floor over to Lord Lechton and Lord Tremaway."

"What is the old man up to now?" Nate wondered. He leapt to his feet and, with Sarah close behind him, hurried back into the ballroom.

11

arah had a bad feeling about this. Nate's father had used one tactic after another to control the son he didn't understand. In the long litany of tyranny, enrolling his only son in the navy in order to remove him from a marriage he had not approved was merely the last and worst example.

Sarah still didn't understand why Nate was back in England, working as a doctor and, if not living with his father, at least on speaking terms with him. But clearly Nate expected another assault on his freedom of choice, and in any conflict between him and the earl, Sarah was on Nate's side.

Lechton was meandering on about his pleasure in the future of his title and his family; about how the 'fruit of his loins' was about to make him very happy. Sarah couldn't see him, but she could hear him, and she could just see Nate, disappearing between shoulders and skirts, making his way to the far end of the room where his father pontificated about the importance of marriage and children and impeccable reputations.

Sarah stopped, her bad feeling coalescing into a nasty suspicion. He sounded as if he was about to announce that she and Nate were married. It was too soon! Nate hadn't told her the rest of his story.

She had avoided telling him about Elias. Besides, her family needed to know before anyone else!

Charlotte came up beside her and linked an arm with hers. "Do you know what is going on?" she whispered.

Sarah shook her head. "I do not. Shh. Let us listen."

Drew touched her arm, a silent support on the other side, and beyond him the duke her uncle. They moved as a group back towards the wall, where they could just see the tops of the two lord's heads, and the face of Lord Framington, standing to one side.

"Here, Lechton," said Lord Tremaway. "My turn. My ladies and my lords, gentlepersons all, I am delighted to announce the betrothal of my daughter, Miss Tremaway, to the son of the Earl of Lechton, Lord Bentham."

Uncle James muttered something under his breath, shooting Sarah a look of alarm. "It isn't true," Sarah told him, her voice drowned in the response from the ball goers—clapping, chatter, and a few cheers, as footmen began to move around with glasses of wine.

Every sound in the room ceased as Nate roared, "No!" in a voice pitched to be heard above a storm. In the tense silence, he must have reached the musicians' platform, for suddenly she could see his head across the crowd. "Miss Tremaway, Lord Tremaway, I regret to inform you that I have not consented to this betrothal. Indeed, I knew nothing of it until you, sir, announced it."

What Sarah could see of Tremaway purpled. "Your father has made a promise, sirrah, and you shall honour it."

"I cannot, my lord, and I will not. My word is already given elsewhere."

Tremaway turned on Lechton, and began shouting about breach of promise, but Lord Framington moved forward and said something to the three angry men. He must have suggested that they take their dispute to a more private setting, for they followed him from the room, and in moments Lady Framington spoke from the platform, her delight at the scandalous doings at her ball only slightly disguised.

"Please let us move on to supper, my friends. It seems the Lechtons and the Tremaways were a little beforehand with their announcement." She giggled. "One must leave them to have their conversation, and await developments!"

"We should go," Uncle James said.

"But Nate—" Sarah protested. "I should wait... We haven't finished our conversation. We were going to have supper together." And she had hoped for a waltz to replace the one they'd missed in order to talk. She yearned to be held in his arms again. But she was being silly. He was unlikely to get out of the trouble his father had fomented in what remained of the evening.

Her sister, as so often, had followed her thoughts. "He will be under intense scrutiny for the rest of the night, Sarah. You know he will. Being seen with him will make you part of the story, too."

The duke nodded, and Sarah could see their point. Until she and Nate knew whether they were married; until they decided what they wished to do about the future; they should avoid making their relationship fodder for the ton's gossip machine.

Tremaway was justly angry. So was Nate, come to that. Miss Tremaway was in tears. Lady Tremaway held her daughter in her arms and glared at Nate. Libby sat on the other side of Miss Tremaway, watching the three men with worried eyes.

Lechton insisted he'd done nothing wrong. "You are my son. You are required to obey me. I told you yesterday that I was choosing a bride for you."

"And I told you," Nate snapped, "that I would not accept any bride you chose. That I could not, because I am already committed."

"No betrothal has been announced," Tremaway complained. "Your match with my daughter has been announced, and your honour demands that you marry her."

"No, Lord Tremaway," Nate said. He would repeat his refusal as often as he needed to do so. He wished he could just tell the man that he was married, but he wouldn't take her choices away from Sarah.

"You have no honour, then," the viscount sneered.

"I have made no agreement with you or your daughter, my lord," Nate pointed out. "My father has given his word, not mine. He does not have the power to give mine. I knew nothing of my father's intentions or yours until you made the announcement. Without my signature, any agreement is unenforceable. You have every right to be angry, but with my father, not with me."

The conversation kept going round and round in circles, Nate alert to cut his father off whenever he was about to mention Sarah's name or the youthful marriage. In the end, Lady Tremaway begged to be allowed to take her daughter home, and the Tremaways retired, still angry.

Lechton went on the attack as soon as they closed the door behind them. "You are a fool, Bentham, allying yourself to the Winshires. Do you know what I heard today? That brat your Sarah Winderfield took out of the workhouse is actually the son of her own sister and brother! Yes, they say Charlotte Winderfield, the one they call a saint, actually seduced her own brother and he killed himself because of it!"

Nate ignored most of that vile nonsense, but he turned to Libby and asked, "Sarah took a boy from the workhouse?"

"Elias, they call him," Libby confirmed, "and it is true that some believe him to be a Winderfield born on the wrong side of the blanket."

Nate felt as if everything in him had come to a stop: his breath, his thoughts, even his heart. He choked out his next question. "How old is Elias?"

The Winshire mansion was mostly in darkness. Nate thought of climbing the fence to check for a back door or an accessible window, but undoubtedly the grounds were patrolled. Nate was willing to back himself in a fair fight, but those guards of Winshire's were trained warriors. His courtship wasn't going to be helped if he annoyed the duke by injuring one of his men, nor did he fancy a beating if he encountered two or more.

Perhaps he should wait until morning. No. He had to speak with Sarah tonight. He knocked on the front door, and was surprised when it was opened by Lord Andrew. The young lord opened the door and waved him in, saying over his shoulder, "You were right, Kaka. Bentham is here. Come in, Bentham. My father said you wouldn't be able to wait until morning."

The duke lounged against a door frame, propped on one shoulder, his arms folded. "My niece has gone up to her suite, Bentham. I take it you wish to speak with her?" He turned to his son. "Drew, would you see if Sarah wishes to come down and talk to Lord Bentham?"

He stepped back and gestured into the room behind him. "If you could indulge me in a couple of answers to questions, Bentham, while we wait for my niece." It was phrased as a question but the tone made it a command.

Nate obeyed, stepping into a comfortably appointed study. "I will answer what I can, Your Grace."

"I am in Lady Sarah's confidence, young man," the duke commented. "Or should I say, Lady Bentham's?"

"That needs to be her choice," Nate said, resisting the primitive surge of possessiveness and pride that wanted to accept the title that proclaimed her his own.

"You will walk away if she chooses not to acknowledge the marriage?"

Nate hesitated. "That was my intention, though I hoped to persuade her to at least allow me to court her again. But I just found out about... Your Grace, the boy? Is he my son?"

"Ah yes. Elias. You will need to talk to Sarah about Elias." He leaned against the desk, steepling his hands and tapping his forefingers against his lips. After a moment, he asked another question. "Can you prove that the marriage took place? Sarah says that is your plan."

"I believe I can, sir. Your brother or my father may have

destroyed the marriage register at Lesser Lechford, but I doubt they knew that the marriage was also recorded at Sutton-Under-Swinwood, where the banns were also called. I believe that made the marriage legal, Your Grace, since my lady was born at and recorded as a resident of Swinwood Hall, and therefore a parishioner at Sutton-Under-Swinwood."

The duke nodded thoughtfully. "I see. And Sutton-Under-Swinwood was even then a refuge for women in hiding, and therefore it was unlikely anyone would speak of the banns to those who might inform my brother or my father."

"Yes, sir. Also, my cousin, if I can find him, may still have my copy of our marriage lines. I do not know, though, whether Lord Sutton or his father obtained an annulment."

The duke inclined his head. "I have seen no evidence of that in the duchy's files. I will ask our solicitors to check their records. I suspect, however, that they would not have wanted the existence of a marriage to be made public. Tell me, if you had come back to find Sarah married again, what would you have done?"

"Nothing, Your Grace. What could I have done without hurting my wife?" That was, in fact, the situation he expected, and the reason he had not wanted to come to London even after he was forced back to England.

"From what I know of my brother and father, they would have gambled on exactly that reaction from you, and left well enough alone. I will check with the solicitors, but I consider it likely there was no annulment."

Nate turned as Sarah spoke from the doorway. "So, we are probably still married," she said, "and certainly were wed all those years ago." She was still in her ball finery, except she had removed her gloves. She came to him with her hands out, and he took them in his.

"I lost faith in you, Nate. I am so sorry."

He gazed down into the beloved eyes, still adjusting to the new difference in perspective. Last time he was this close, he had not reached his full adult height. "You had cause, dearest heart." The endearment he had always used came easily back to his tongue.

"You are not to blame. Forgive me for giving up on reaching you with word of my survival? For not coming back to you as soon as I was free?"

"We shall forgive one another, then," Sarah said. She looked down, pressing her lips between the teeth, that endearing little crease between her brows deepening.

"You can say to me anything you wish," Nate prompted.

She met his eyes, then. "Can I? I do not know you now. You do not know me. We have both changed in seven years, Nate. How could we not? You call me 'dearest heart', but how can you love someone you do not know?"

It was a fair question. Nate frowned in his turn, trying to find the right words. "I know I admire what I have heard of you, Sarah. I know I want you—more, I think, than I did when we were wed, though my younger self would not have believed that possible. You have my respect and my desire, which is a good start, I think?"

Sarah had to acknowledge the point. In fairness, she should admit to her body's response. It bothered and confused her. In seven years, she had convinced herself that her memory of their reaction to one another must be false; that she was, by nature, cold, for she had met many attractive men since she entered Society, and none of them moved her in the slightest.

She heated to melting point when she saw him on the other side of a room. Standing so close, her hands in his, it was taking all the discipline she had to keep from draping herself over him and demanding that he did something about the fire he had ignited.

Uncle James! They had been standing here almost embracing. What must her uncle think of her? But when she looked around for him, he was nowhere to be seen, and the door she had left open behind her was closed.

"Sarah," Nate said, "I am willing to court you, to give you time to know me again. I was prepared to walk away, if that was your choice, though it would be like tearing my heart out all over again. But what of Elias?"

It is because of Elias that I must be sure. Sarah tried to pull her hands away, but he held on, firmly but gently. She couldn't think of anything to say except, "You know."

"I only found out about him this evening, when my father tossed the fact of his existence at me as an argument against you. He thinks you are covering up the sins of your sister, but as soon as I heard, I knew." His fingers relaxed and his jaw firmed. "Did you not intend to tell me?"

This time, she did pull loose, and turned away to hide her flush. "I wanted time." Time to find out if this new harder version of the boy she had loved would be kind; to find out if Nate could be trusted.

It seemed they were truly married, which increased the risk. As Sarah's husband and Elias's father, he had every legal right to take his son. She could trust her family to fight for her freedom if she found marriage to Nate unbearable, but in that case, she would lose Elias. She could not imagine Nate had become brutal enough that the courts of England would not find in his favour if they fought over custody.

She chanced a glance back at him, to see how angry he was, and was disarmed by his thoughtful nod. "You wanted to protect our son. I can respect that. I am not a danger to him, dearest heart, nor to you. I will give you the time you need to find that out."

He rubbed at the back of his neck. He used to do that when he was much younger, when he was deeply moved and concerned, and trying to hide it. "You have been looking for a husband this Season, they tell me. Were you looking for love? Or for a companionable marriage?"

Sarah noted the past tense but didn't challenge it. He was right, of course. Her husband hunt was over. She gave Nate the truth. "I was seeking a father for Elias."

Nate spread his hands. "Then let me show I can be what you both need," he begged.

He was asking when he had the right to demand. That was in

his favour. Hard as Sarah found it to trust anyone other than Charlotte, he deserved the chance he asked for. "Shall we start with a meeting in St James Park tomorrow? At the Chinese Bridge?" she asked. "Elias likes to feed the ducks."

His smile lit his eyes and softened every line of his face. "I would like that. Shall I see if Libby and my sisters would like to join me? We should avoid a public show of our... connection. Just while Society is getting over my father's mad start, and while you are deciding our future."

He was right, and his willingness to avoid forcing her hand added another mark to his credit. "Tell Lady Lechton to bring bread," she advised. "Shall we say noon?"

"Shall we say Fournier's afterwards, for some of his little cakes?" Nate countered.

"I expect your sisters would enjoy that," Sarah teased.

He lifted a quizzical eyebrow. "Have you lost your sweet tooth, then, dearest heart?"

She shook her head. "I am as bad as ever, I fear."

His murmured, "One can hope," was not meant to be heard, and he tried to cover by saying aloud, "Fournier's, then." The enterprising Marcel Fournier was a darling of the Polite World, and had recently opened a pastry shop to complement his *restaurant*.

"Until tomorrow." Sarah gave in to the impulse to offer him her hands again, and this time he pulled her close and lowered his head, stopping when his lips were no more than an inch from hers. She waited a moment. He stayed where he was, the terrible man. Sarah raised herself that inch, her mouth tentative on his.

Odd. She thought she remembered his kisses. But she had forgotten the sweetness of it, the way his lips softened, the touch of his tongue asking her to open, the way he stroked into her mouth. With each moment, as the kiss deepened and his gentle persuasion became more insistent, more urgent, the memories flooded back.

That summer, they had discovered a hundred ways to kiss, a thousand. Different touches, different pressures, different positions. This, hand in hand, nothing but their mouths connected, was tame compared to some of their explorations, but there was nothing tame about the impact.

Cold? She could do with some cold. A dip in ice would not put out the conflagration.

When he pulled away, she whimpered.

His voice was strained as he stepped back, using his grasp on her hands to hold her at arm's-length. "Dearest heart, have mercy. I am on fire, and if you are not going to invite me to stay..."

Oh. Her face heated. She dropped her gaze to his fall and blinked.

"Indeed," he confirmed, with a short laugh. "I thought I had acquired considerable control over these past seven years, but you are fast demolishing it, my lady. Let me wish you a good night while I am still sane enough to be a gentleman."

He was correct again, though for a wild moment she had not been able to think of any reason not to invite him to continue what they'd started. "Tomorrow, then," she managed.

Nate gave her hands a final squeeze and released them. "Tomorrow," he confirmed, with a bow.

Sarah followed him to the door and watched him cross the entrance hall where a footman waited to let him out. *Four*, she said to herself as the door closed behind him. *One more point for that kiss, and another for stopping.*

12

Nate couldn't persuade Libby to accompany him. "I cannot come with you," she kept saying.

He explained that he needed her and the children to cover his purpose in being there. "If I turn up on my own near the children and the ducks, and start talking to the Winderfield party, it will be all over town within the hour," he pointed out.

"Lord Lechton does not wish to acknowledge the marriage, Nate," Libby said. "I cannot come with you, Bentham. I am sorry."

"Lord Lechton will change his mind when he realises what this means," Nate assured her, though he did wonder. The old man was not flexible in his thinking. "His heir already has a legitimate heir. He has achieved his goal."

"Perhaps." Libby was even more doubtful than Nate. "But we cannot ask him, for he went out after you argued yesterday evening, and has not come home. I cannot come with you."

He could not push her further. She was right that his father's wrath would fall unequally, since there wasn't much he could do to Nate, but Libby was fully in the old reprobate's power. "Do not concern yourself, Libby. I will think of something else."

"Take the girls." Libby looked surprised by her own suggestion, but took a deep breath and repeated it. "Yes. Take the girls. Lechton cannot blame *me* if *you* take the girls to the park and happen to meet Lady Sarah. How would I know your intention?" She blushed, bright scarlet. "You must think me dreadful, to suggest deceiving my husband."

"On the contrary," Nate reassured her. "I think you a brave sweet lady, doing her best by your husband's son. Yes, and Lechton, too, for he will only make a fool of himself if he goes up against the will of the Duke of Winshire, and the duke has accepted me as Sarah's husband."

Libby's eyes widened. "Truly? Then you must go to the park, Bentham. Indeed, I must say I think it very wicked to separate a husband and wife, even if you were a disobedient son to marry Lady Sarah against your father's wishes. But if the marriage is real, then there is nothing further to be said." She gave a determined nod. "Indeed, it is my duty to help you and your wife. Take your sisters to the park, my lord. I shall tell their nurse and the governess."

"Say nothing of my marriage for the moment, Libby, if you please. I have promised Lady Sarah time to consider whether she wishes it to be known."

Libby's eyes rounded. "She might refuse to remain married, you mean? But divorce would ruin her, Bentham."

"Let us hope it does not come to that. Indeed, I am hopeful that I can win her again, and I certainly mean to try. For I tell you, Libby, if I cannot win my wife back, I will never marry."

"Oh dear," Libby responded. "I will say nothing, then, but I do wish you every success."

As a result, Nate found himself escorting a bevy of females to the Chinese Bridge in St James Park. Honoria, aged five, walked beside him, holding his hand. The nurse followed, with three-year-old Lavinia in her arms, with the nursemaid pushing the baby carriage containing little Phillida, most commonly known as Baby. A footman trailed the party, carrying the essential bags of stale bread and buns, and another carried umbrellas in case the hovering clouds turned to rain.

Built for the victory celebrations earlier that year, the Chinese
Bridge had fallen victim to the fireworks it had hosted for the occa-
sion. It still stood, though fire scorched, but the pagoda that had
been the centrepiece was gone.

Sarah and her sister had chosen a spot just along the bank of
the canal. Lord Andrew was in attendance. A nursemaid stood back
with several of the Winderfield guard. But Nate only had eyes for
Sarah and the boy. Elias. His son. He was breaking chunks of bread
off a loaf and tossing it to a squabbling rabble of ducks, and Sarah
was right beside him, laughing at the birds' antics, pointing to ducks
that had been shouldered to the outskirts, and making comments
that had Elias tipping back his head to shout with laughter.

Nate shepherded his entourage to the side of the Winderfield
party, and nodded to the footman to distribute the bread to the two
older girls. Baby was sound asleep in her carriage.

Lord Andrew opened the conversation between the two parties.
"Good day, Bentham. Your sisters, I take it?"

"Lady Honoria Beauclair and Lady Lavinia with the ducks."
Nate broke off to swoop Lavie up into his arms as half a dozen
ducks at once tried to pull the bread from her arms, and she opened
her mouth to roar. "A little bit at a time, sweetheart," he told her,
demonstrating as he settled her safely on one arm.

"And Lady Phillida asleep in the carriage," he added.

Lady Charlotte was staring at Norie. "My goodness, Sarah,
Lady Honoria and El—your ward could be brother and sister."

She was right. They had the same colouring, the same lean
frame and oval face, the same determined chin and straight brows
with a downward hook at the end. Elias's hair was cropped short,
but still showed a tendency to curl, as did Norie's under her pretty
cloth bonnet.

He exchanged a smile with Sarah. No one would remain in
doubt of Elias's parentage when they saw the two children together.

Elias tugged on Sarah's hand. "I need more bread, Mama."

"We have lots of bread," Norie offered. "I can give the boy some
bread, can I not, Bentham?"

Elias stared at her for a moment, his eyes wide, then remembered his manners. "Thank you, miss. But Uncle Drew has more bread." He seemed to think this an adequate introduction, because he added, "You should throw some to that one at the back. The others are being greedy."

Norie threw a piece of bread over the heads of the other ducks. It fell short, and before the target duck could read it, it was mobbed in a flurry of beaks and wings.

"They stole it," Norie noted, then stamped a foot. "Bad ducks! You have no manners."

"Ducks have duck manners," observed Elias, from all the superiority of a year's age and masculinity. "Here, let me help you."

He took position beside the little girl, and showed her how to make pellets of the bread so they flew more accurately, and they were soon making a game of picking a duck to favour with their largesse and then throwing to that duck, groaning when another web-toed bandit reached the morsel first and cheering when they succeeded.

"He is a kind boy," Nate observed to Sarah, blinking a little to clear the moisture from his eyes. "Me too, Benth," Lavie demanded, wriggling to be put down. "Me throw bread with Boy."

He set her on the ground and she rushed to squeeze between her sister and Elias—her nephew, Nate thought with bemusement— all the better to be protected from the ducks. Elias smiled down at her. "Is this your sister?" he asked Norie.

"She's Lavie. And I'm Norie. And there's Baby, too, but she's asleep." Norie waved in the direction of the carriage without looking away from the ducks.

"Bwead, Norie," Lavie demanded.

Elias gave her a pelleted morsel. "Throw it over the ducks," he advised. "I'm Elias," he told Norie. "Pleased to meet you."

Lavie's effort flew all of two feet. Elias squatted on his heels to give Lavie another piece of bread, and showed her how to swing her arm so it flew at least four feet, right into the clamouring flock.

Nate's eyes were watering again. What a fine little lad he was!

"Will you tell me about him?" he asked Sarah, who had slipped her hand into the crook of his elbow, and was having a similar problem with her tear ducts as she watched the children.

Lord Andrew and Lady Charlotte had moved to the other side of the children, the servants had fallen back to cluster around the baby carriage, and the guard maintained their watchfulness in a semicircle around their charges. They were as private as they could be in such a public place.

"He is a kind boy, as you have said. Quiet, but he is coming out of his shell as he gains confidence. Very clever, too. In the eight months since I found him, he has almost caught up with his age group in most of his subjects, and is reading beyond what his nurse-maid expects."

"Only eight months? Rumour has it you found him in a workhouse."

"His foster parents died, and their family didn't want him. He was there only four months, Nate, but you should have seen him. He was skin and bones, and so nervous."

Nate didn't know what to say. The thought of his son being abused set his every protective instinct into full emergency action, and it was all too late. A year ago, he had been in Edinburgh, still under naval discipline, but he could have asked for leave in between terms. He could have come looking for his wife, and if he had, he might have been able to rescue his son before the poor little man was hurt.

"I lost them, Nate. Mama hand-picked them, and I think they were good to Elias, for he remembers them fondly. But my grandfa-ther paid them to move away, and to break their agreement to send Mama reports on Elias's health. We didn't know where they had gone, and my grandfather was not telling." She wiped away a tear.

"I tried, Nate. I saved as much as I could from my pin money, and I spent it all on hiring a man to search for Elias. But he found nothing. He kept asking for more money, but there was none. No more pin money and my dowry was gone—not that my father would have given it to me, even if my grandfather and father had not spent it all."

"But you persisted, and in the end, you found him."

"Uncle James came, and all of a sudden I had a bigger allowance than I had ever had in my life. I decided to try a new agent. I don't think the first one ever left London. He just took my money and lied to me about what he was doing. But Prue—Mrs Wakefield—wouldn't give up. And in the end, she found Elias and brought him to me."

Nate put his hand over the one tucked into his elbow and stroked. "You have him now. You missed those years when he was little, years in which you could have known him and loved him, but he is here now. You have the future."

She smiled up at him. "We have the future. I'll not keep him from you, Nate." She focused her eyes on his cravat pin, veiling them with her lashes. "I'll not keep either us from you."

He bent his head closer. "Unfair to tell me that now, in public, where I am constrained from kissing you."

"I didn't mean to, yet," Sarah admitted. "But the loving way you treat your sisters, and then you said that about my future, not assuming that we would be together...and I can see how much Elias moves you. We are married, Nate, in intention, whatever the law says. I do not know you well any more. But I know you can be trusted with my son. I know you are a decent, honourable man."

She coloured. "I know I desire you, as I have not desired any man since the last time we were together. Perhaps that would not be quite enough if we were not already married. But we are, and I do not want to waste any more time when we have already lost seven years. Unless you are not ready?"

"Ready?" Nate's grin must have been visible from St James Palace, it was so wide. "Dearest heart, I cannot wait to tell the whole world that you are my wife and Elias is my son. And to make a home with the pair of you." Now there was a disturbing thought. "I cannot take you to my lodgings. We shall have to find a place to live."

"Yes, and we need to tell Elias, and work out how to announce our marriage to the world."

"It would also be helpful if I can bring my father around.

Which, since his greatest ambition is to have a grandson, is looking increasingly possible."

"We have some work to do, then, my darling." She smiled up at him, and he desperately wanted to lean under her very fetching hat and kiss her, but just then Norie screeched, "But I want to go on the bridge!"

Her nurse, who was unfortunately as timid as Libby, was making ineffectual noises, but Elias said firmly, "You cannot, Norie. It is not safe. My mama says it caught fire, and it might collapse if we go on it. Then the fishes will nibble your toes, and you would not like that."

Norie narrowed her eyes.

"Go on bwidge," Lavie demanded.

"Go to the tea shop for cake," Nate suggested, swinging her back up into his arms, and the distraction worked magnificently. "Would you like to join us for cake, Master Elias? You and your family?"

13

Elias opened his mouth to reply then shut it. Sarah was pleased to see him remember his manners. "May we, Mama?"

At Sarah's nod, he managed a creditable bow. "Yes, please, sir."

"To Fournier's, then," Nate said, and shared a smile with Sarah when the boy offered his arm to Norie in imitation of his elders. Charlotte grinned at Sarah and took Drew's arm.

What a procession they made!

Drew and Charlotte led the way, with Elias and Norie next and then Nate and Sarah with Lavie still enthroned on Nate's other arm.

The cluster of nursemaids followed with Phillida still in her baby carriage but now awake and chattering in baby gurgles at everything they passed.

The footmen brought up the rear and the guard spread out on both sides of the path.

Quite a sight, if somewhat wasted on the noontime park crowd of children and their nursemaids, off-duty soldiers, and scurrying citizens using the park as a thoroughfare between Westminster and Mayfair.

Fournier's was a short stroll away. It was still early afternoon,

well before the fashionable promenade hours, and the pastry shop
had only just opened. Nate commandeered a table large enough for
the family, and another for the servants and guard, and suggested
that everyone order what they most desired.

They had a wonderful time, and Sarah fell in love a little bit
more with this new, more mature version of Nate, as he discussed
different types of waterfowl with Elias, fed morsels of sweet cake to
his smallest sister, answered question after question from Norie, and
gently encouraged Norie and Elias to give Lavie her chance to have
her say from time to time, though most of what she said was unintelligible, at least to Sarah.

When the topic turned to horses, Nate disclaimed any expertise.
"I have been at sea since I was seventeen," he explained, "but Lord
Andrew knows all about them."

Norie turned to Drew with her question, and while the children
were distracted, Sarah asked hers. "Where did you learn to be so
good with children?"

"All it takes is patience and the willingness to listen. Much like
medicine, in fact. I boarded with a widow and her eight children in
Edinburgh," Nate explained. "Mrs McTavish tried to keep them out
of my way to start with, but I enjoyed them. Fascinating little
beings. One doesn't see many children aboard a warship."

"Hello," said a familiar voice. Drew's sister Ruth had just
entered the shop, with her husband Val and his two daughters.

"Have you come to take tea? Join us," Charlotte suggested, then
cast a guilty look at Nate, who was their host. "If you do not mind,
Lord Bentham."

"Lord Bentham!" Ruth exclaimed. "Val, remember Lord
Bentham, the volunteer doctor who worked so hard the day of the
fire?"

While the two men were shaking hands, Ruth cast a glance
around the table. "And who do we have here?" Her eyes caught on
Norie, and she looked from the girl to Elias and then back again,
before raising her eyebrows at Sarah.

"Lord Bentham's younger sisters, Ruth. Please allow me to
present Lady Honoria, Lady Lavinia, and Lady Phillida Beauclair."

Ruth's eyebrows elevated still further, and she nodded, smiling at Nate and exhaling with an "Aaah."

Sarah ignored her, continuing the introductions. "Young ladies, say good afternoon to Lord and Lady Ashbury. Lady Ashbury is Lord Andrew's sister." She gestured to Ashbury's two girls. "And these are Lady Mirabel and Lady Genevieve Ashbury."

"Please, do join us," Nate invited, and he gestured to one of the shop servants to bring over another table and some more chairs.

They shuffled around, so that the children had their own table, all except Phillida, who stayed on her brother's knee. Ruth was clearly bursting with questions, and Sarah was sure Val had noticed the resemblance, though he, too, did not remark on it.

Still, that was three people who had noticed how much alike Elias and Norie were. If Sarah had learned anything from the gossip that had swirled around the Winderfields in the past few years, it was that the only way to come out on top was to give Society a story of which they approved, and preferably to make that story public before someone else made the narrative scandalous.

They were running out of time.

This was confirmed before they left the pastry shop, when Madame Fournier, wife of the chef and a distant cousin of the Duchess of Haverford, came over to greet them.

Sarah introduced Nate. The twins and Cecilia Fournier had become friends over the last two years as they worked together on various charities, and she had already met the Winderfield cousins. Like Ruth, her eyes tracked from Elias to Norie and back again.

Cecilia was the soul of discretion and would say nothing. They could not count on the next person being so discreet. She and Nate needed to talk to Elias before somebody else did.

The two parties separated after Fournier's, the Winderfields going in one direction, the Ashburys in another and Nate and his party in a third. Norie and Lavie chatted about Elias and the pretty ladies. Too full of his own thoughts, Nate heard little of what they said. He'd missed seven years of marriage; six years of his son's life. Sarah and Elias, too, had been robbed of the years together they should have had.

He had engaged to take Sarah driving tomorrow during the fashionable afternoon strut in Hyde Park—another public move in a courting that fretted at his nerves. He wanted to be with them now, to tell the world that Sarah was his wife, Elias his son.

He had promised her time, but they'd already lost so much. He knew his own heart; and he believed Sarah now knew hers. But he had agreed to let her set the pace, and would keep his promise.

He saw the girls to the nursery, gave Libby a brief and insubstantial report of the outing, and escaped to an appointment with Wakefield, the private enquiry agent who was related to the Marquis of Aldridge.

"I know you are busy investigating the arson at the clinic," he apologised, once he had explained why he needed to find his father's cousin, and answered all of Wakefield's questions. "Next to that, this probably does not seem urgent. A few days delay after all these years..." He shrugged, while the urge to demand instant results beat within him.

"I do have a few interviews to carry out regarding the various attacks—you know that the fire was only one of many incidents?" Wakefield raised his brows in question, then continued at Nate's nod. "The agents and informers on my payroll are carrying out most of the work, and we're also co-operating with several magistrate's offices across London and Westminster. It does not require most of my attention. I can look into your little problem immediately."

Nate smiled his relief.

Wakefield steepled his forefingers and touched them to his lower lip, for a moment resembling his more prestigious brother. "I will send someone to Oxfordshire to look at the records," he decided. "I imagine we'll find a missing page in the parish register at Lesser Lechford, but I wonder if he thought to check the one at Sutton-Under-Swinwood? It is worth looking. Also, since you were living with your cousin, some of the local people may remember the wedding, or at least the reading of the banns. It would have been an event in their lives, the marriage of the curate's much younger cousin."

Nate nodded. That all made sense, and he'd thought of doing it himself; would do it, if he didn't feel the urgent need to be here in London, where Sarah was.

"As to finding your cousin, I have several ideas about that. Leave it with me, Lord Bentham. I will be in touch as soon as I have anything to report."

Nate had to be satisfied with that, and left for the temporary clinic that the Ashburys had set up in an empty building owned by the Duke of Winshire. Perhaps work would help to subdue, or at least redirect, the urge to action. But deep down, he was sure that time was running out.

He went out the next morning to buy a curricle and pair. If he was going to take the Diamond of the *ton* driving, he was not going to embarrass her with a hired carriage and a pair of slugs from a livery stable. Then he had to find stabling and a carriage house. By the time all was organised, he had an hour until their outing, during which he needed to return to his rooms to change his clothing.

His usual casual approach to attire had been shaken by contrast with the always impeccable Marquis of Aldridge. He would swear that it was Charlotte who had attracted the marquis's eye, and certainly Sarah was no more than friendly to the man, but still. Nate was courting, after all. He should look the part. It was his man's half-day, which made it more complicated.

He hurried up the stairs to his rooms, stopping a maid on the way to ask for a jug of hot water. As he opened his door, he was running through the cravat knots he'd learned, and wondering if the gentleman in the rooms next door, who had taught him most of them, might be home to assist.

He pulled up short when he saw his visitor. His father sat in one of the chairs by the fire, looking up as Nate entered. "Is it true?"

No point in wasting time berating Lechton for bulldozing his way into his rooms, or the landlord for allowing it. Nate put his hat and gloves down on the side table just inside the door, and shrugged out of his coat. "You will excuse me if I wash and change while we talk, my lord. I have an afternoon engagement."

Lechton waved a hand in dismissal or agreement; Nate hardly cared which. "Libby told me you went to meet Lady Sarah today—"

Nate turned from the drawer that held his best shirts and glared at the old man. "If you have come to berate me, I do not wish to hear it."

"No, no..." The old man trailed off at the knock on the door.

Nate opened it and took the jug of hot water and the landlord's stammered explanation that the gentleman insisted on waiting for him in his rooms. "And he is an earl, my lord, and your father, so I thought—"

"No harm done," Nate told him, "as long as you do not make a habit of it."

He crossed to the washstand and poured some of the water into the bowl.

Lechton started again. "Libby told me... No, don't poker up, Bentham. You need to listen to me."

Nate pulled his shirt off over his head and soaped his washcloth. "Say what you came to say, my lord."

"Is it true that Lady Sarah's ward is your son? Yours and hers?"

The cold burn that had been simmering since he discovered Elias's existence flared into anger as he spun to fix his father with furious eyes. "My son! Born to my wife, in grief and shame because you and Sutton tore us apart. Given to others to raise and only rescued because my wife did not give up looking for him. I have struggled these seven years to forgive you, Father, as Jesus teaches, but what you did to Sarah, to Elias... I don't know if I can ever forgive you for that."

Lechton shrunk in his chair, the colour bleaching out of his face. "But Nathaniel, I did not know."

Nate focused on his breathing, struggling to overcome the urge to hit something, preferably his father. He didn't know? What kind of an excuse was that? Under control again, he turned back to the washbasin.

"I have an engagement, my lord, so if that is all...?"

Lechton sounded unaccountably meek, even a little frightened. "Sutton told me you would not be harmed. He said you had to go, and an annulment would be easier if I agreed to sign the papers for you to be enlisted in the navy. He said if I did not sign, he would make his daughter a widow. What was I to do, Bentham? Winshire held my living. I feared I would be thrown out in the street and you would be dead."

You could have stood up to them. You could have warned me and Sarah so we could run. You could have refused to tell them how to find us. All of these thoughts surged through Nate's mind, but what was the point in saying any of them? For better or for worse, his father's decisions had been made. They couldn't change the past. "I nearly was dead. I spent the first week of the voyage unconscious, and the next month recovering from broken ribs and bruised organs."

"They said you would not be harmed," Lechton repeated. "I… I am sorry I never answered your letters, Bentham. When I was told you had died in a naval action—I have always regretted that I never replied to your letters."

Nate turned to lean against the washstand as he dried his face, throat, torso and arms. *Father thought me dead?* Another thing to blame Sarah's grandfather for, he supposed.

Lechton hadn't finished. "I do not wish to offend, but are you sure the boy is your son, Bentham?"

Nate swallowed his howl of outrage, and returned a short answer. "Yes."

Lechton wouldn't let it go. "Libby tells me he looks just like Honoria; enough alike to be a brother, the nursemaid told her, apparently."

"Well, then."

"The duke said the marriage was not valid, but Cousin Arthur insisted... Well. I was just thinking, if you and Lady Sarah are married, and Elias is your son... I was thinking..."

"The marriage is almost certainly valid. The current duke has consulted his lawyers. They are checking precedent, but it makes no difference what they decide, my lord. Sarah is my wife, and I'll have no other. If the lawyers are uncertain of the legality of the wedding, and if Sarah agrees to have me, we will marry again."

Lechton purpled and half stood. "Agrees to have you? You are an earl's heir. Of course, she will have you. No, the marriage must stand. We must prove that it was valid." He smiled. "A grandson. I have a legitimate grandson. An heir to my heir. Fruit of my loins."

Nate interrupted. "You will not interfere in any way, Lord Lechton. Sarah has given me permission to court her, and the Duke of Winshire has insisted that it is to be her choice. I have promised I will not speak of it until she gives me leave. I warn you, if you let out word of our marriage before Sarah is ready to accept it, you are likely to send her fleeing back to Winds' Gate and neither I nor Winshire will let that happen without repercussions."

Lechton subsided back into the chair. "Court her? Your own wife! But if the duke chooses to support her..." He shook his head.

Nate pulled on a clean shirt and tucked it into his pantaloons. "Why the change of tune?" At his father's blank expression, he elucidated. "You said Lady Sarah was unsuitable; tried to force me into a betrothal with Miss Tremaway." He sat down to pull on clean stockings.

Lechton shook his head as if he couldn't believe Nate didn't understand. "A bird in the hand, Bentham. She already has your son. A growing boy past the age of infant diseases. The Tremaway chit or any other untried girl might be infertile or—Heaven help us —produce only daughters, like my Libby. No, no. We don't need Miss Tremaway. Nathaniel, I could not be more pleased. I have a grandson! Are you making an afternoon call? Have you sent flowers? Not the green waistcoat, boy; the blue one with the silver embroidery is more elegant. Here, let me do your cravat."

Nate allowed him to take over the folding and arranging of the stupid thing, and had to concede that Lechton did a good job of it, even donating his own cravat pin to the cause.

"I am taking Lady Sarah for a drive," he admitted, when

Lechton asked again whether he would be visiting the lady, and Lechton nodded, well pleased. He remained as Nate finished dressing, clucking over the choice of boots, admiring Nate's new jacket.

"Invite your wife to dinner," he suggested. "I will go home and tell Lady Lechton. A private family meal, that's the ticket."

"I do not wish to rush her," Nate pointed out. "Pushing my family on her this early might frighten her away." Lord Lechton might frighten her away. She had already met the children, and Libby was a sweet timid little thing who would never scare anyone.

"Invite her," Lechton insisted. "Let her have the choice. Is that not what you said?"

They walked out together, and Lechton followed Nate to the mews where his new curricle waited, the horses gleaming in their new harness. "Invite her," he said again. "Please? I want... I would like to hear about my grandson. Perhaps we could visit. Do you think we could visit?"

Nate said something noncommittal about it being up to Sarah, and managed to get away. How ironic that, now he no longer cared whether or not he pleased his father, he had finally achieved it, all unknowing.

14

Sarah was rather more understanding about Lechton's about-face than Nate. "He betrayed you, Nate, but surely it makes you feel better to know it was in order to save your life? Indeed, when I think about what might have happened, I am glad they thought to send you into the navy, where you were far, far away when I refused to co-operate with their plans to marry me off."

She shuddered. If her father and grandfather had decided to make her a widow, if she had been presented with Nate's body, would she have been strong enough to stand out against them? In those early days, she had been sure he would return; certain that he loved her and that love would conquer everything.

She smiled at the thought. And now it seemed she had been right.

Nate did not look convinced. "What you and Elias went through... I should have been here to help you, Sarah. To support and love you."

"You are here now. And I want to know all about you, Nate. Where have you been? What have you done? What made you decide to become a doctor?"

Conversation had been easy for them from the beginning, and

today Sarah found that hadn't changed. He answered those questions and asked his own, which led to more questions from them both, as the minutes flew by.

Nate drove them into the far reaches of Hyde Park, away from the fashionable carriage way. Two of her uncle's guard kept pace at a distance, but didn't disturb them. However, they were not entirely left alone. They were interrupted frequently by acquaintances wanting to greet Sarah and stare at Nate.

Still, they had each related the major elements of their separate journeys to this place and time when the sun touched the horizon and they woke up to the fact that the day was over and cold night was approaching.

Nate turned the horses for the gate nearest to Winshire House, and set them trotting, and the guard closed in to follow. "May I see you again tomorrow, my love?" Nate asked.

Long ago, Sarah had thrown her heart over the moon, and run off to marry Nate. For years, she'd mourned that decision, believing he'd played her false. But it wasn't true. He had been trustworthy then; he was trustworthy now. It was time to take another leap in faith.

"If Uncle James is free tonight, do you think Lady Lechton would mind two more for dinner? I think we should discuss our plans to announce our marriage."

The horses checked as Nate tightened his hands, turning to her with such joy and heat in his eyes that she nearly threw herself into his arms, and only refrained because she looked behind her at that moment and saw the guardsmen, and other riders, heading home in the gathering dusk. They were in a public place, but soon enough, they would be alone. Her centre melted at the thought.

"It is time, do you not think?" she asked.

"I promised to wait until you are ready," he reminded her, setting the horses back into an easy pace towards the gate. His voice vibrated with delight as he added, "And if you are ready, my love, I can only thank God for it, for I cannot sleep or think for wanting you."

The dinner went well, Sarah thought. Lord Lechton was beside himself with glee at the sudden expansion of his family, and in the mood to be expansively hospitable. The others at the table had to intervene several times to keep him from talking about the marriage and Elias in front of the servants.

When the last course was served, Nate stepped in, suggesting that they dismiss the servants for the time being, and Lechton leapt at the notion. "Yes! Yes indeed, my boy. Barker, that will be all. We shall serve ourselves. I will let you know when you can clear!"

The butler bowed and ushered the footmen from the room, shutting the door behind them, and the true business of the evening began.

"When shall we announce the marriage?" Lechton demanded. "Can I meet my grandson tomorrow? You shall move in with us, Lady Bentham. We have the room, do we not, Lady Lechton? My grandson shall like sharing a nursery with his aunts."

Uncle James took the conversation in hand, before Nate could speak the hasty words Sarah could see on his tongue. "You will wish Elias to be accepted as your legitimate grandson with as little scandal as possible, Lechton, so we shall proceed with caution this week, sowing the seeds. We shall make the formal announcement at a ball I shall hold at Winshire House at the end of the week. I have already written to my sister and sister-in-law asking them to come to London to give the young couple their support."

Lechton took a gulp of his wine as he thought about that. "Yes. Yes, of course, Your Grace. I see your point."

Sarah tried the same calm, firm tone to address the other issue. "Nate and I have not yet discussed where we will live, Lord Lechton, but we will, of course, enjoy visiting family."

Lechton dismissed her remark with an airy wave. "You are my son's wife. You will live with me, of course."

"No," Nate said. Just that. Nothing more.

Lechton purpled. "Now look here, Bentham."

Nate put up a hand in a stop gesture. "We will not require your support, if that is your concern. And our living arrangements are not up for discussion, my lord. Sarah and I will make our own decision."

"I agree," Uncle James said. "You have lost seven years together, and your families owe you their support to live your lives in the way you choose."

Lechton subsided at that, and Uncle James moved smoothly to discussing what activities the Benthams, as he called Sarah and Nate, might engage in during the next few days.

By the time they left the dining table, Sarah and Nate had agreed that they would talk to Elias together the next day, and introduce him to Lord and Lady Lechton afterwards. They would attend the Opera in the Duke of Winshire's box tomorrow night, and ride in Hyde Park each day for the rest of the week.

Further, at Sarah's suggestion, she and Nate would visit the Tremaways to explain their history before the announcement at the ball. That should help to make peace between Tremaway and Lechton.

The ball at the end of the week would be a glittering finale to the year. Uncle James was certain they would get excellent attendance, and Sarah didn't doubt it. Her mother and aunt, and her godmother, the Duchess of Haverford, would see to that.

Once they were settled in the drawing room with the tea tray, the conversation turned to proving the validity of the marriage. Nate described his conversation with Wakefield. "We may have results from Oxfordshire in time for the ball," he said, "but I don't know how long it will take to get news of my cousin."

Lechton's brows shot up. "But I can tell you that. Winshire put pressure on our mutual cousin who was earl before me to get rid of the man. He was only a curate, you know. I lost track of him for a while, but the solicitors found him again when the previous earl died. He is my heir after you, you know. After Elias, now."

"You said you know where he is?" Nate asked.

"Why, not more than an hour's drive from here, in the village of Hounswood. He is curate to the vicar of St Chad's. I... um... we do not talk. But he would talk to you, Nate. He always felt that you were in the right back then, and were badly treated."

Sarah could see Nate swallowing a sharp answer before he asked, politely, for his cousin's direction, and Lechton went off to his study to find it.

"What an astounding coincidence, Nate. St Chad's in Hounswood sponsors the training centre I told you about: The Theodora Foundation. I might have met him myself if I had taken the women Charlotte rescued to deliver them to the village. But apparently Aldridge is going to Kent, and has promised to detour past Hounswood, so their travel is all organised."

Sarah and Nate left the Lechton townhouse not long after. "Shall we drop you off, Bentham?" Uncle James asked.

Sarah took a deep breath and said, "Can we go past Nate's rooms so he can get a change for the morning, Uncle James? I would like him to come home with me." By the time she had finished the sentence, her face was burning, and the heat had spread even to her ears and her throat.

But Nate's broad smile and the warmth in his eyes made it all worthwhile, and Uncle James didn't turn a hair. "Certainly." And he turned to give the instruction to his coachman.

The servants would not talk. Their enemies had ensured that. In the last two and a half years, Sarah's cousin Sutton and Yousef, her uncle's aide, had tested and confirmed the loyalty of everyone who worked in one of their households. Not everyone in England approved of a mixed-race ducal family, and they had suffered every-thing from gossip to assassination attempts.

Here, in Sarah's own home, she and Nate could begin their marriage again without word leaking before they were ready.

Even so, she led him, her hand in his, up a secondary staircase to the suite she shared with her sister. As soon as she opened the door, she knew Charlotte was home early. The wrap Charlotte had worn was thrown over the back of a sofa, and the door to Charlotte's chamber was open. She could not see the bed from this angle, but Charlotte's maid Clarke moved around the room, snuffing the candles.

Sarah drew Nate into the room and shut the door behind them. "I will just check on my sister. Would you care for a brandy?" She gestured to the decanters. "Help yourself. I won't be moment."

"Do you wish me to go?" he asked.

She had already taken two paces across the room but at that she turned back. She reached up to his face with her palm, kissing his other cheek. "I want you to stay. Will you stay, Nate?"

His eyes devoured her as he nodded, and the heat rose in her again. *Charlotte. I am going to check on Charlotte.* She stiffened her shaking knees, and crossed the room to Charlotte's chamber.

"Her ladyship is right poorly tonight," Clarke whispered. "The usual trouble."

The heap of blankets on the bed shifted. "Is that you, Sarah?" Her voice was barely louder than the maid's. When Charlotte's indisposition approached, it began with a headache that only worsened as the other cramps and aches descended upon her. "You are home early."

"And I have a guest, my dear. Nate is with me. Clarke, Lord Bentham is in the sitting room. He will be staying the night." The maid's training held good; her reaction confined to widened eyes and a dropped jaw that she closed immediately. "Congratulate me. You are the first outside of immediate family to know that I am married."

Clarke curtsied in her confusion, and stammered, "I am about done here, my lady." Her head came up at a knock on the outside door. "That will be Lady Charlotte's brick." She curtsied again. "Please excuse me, my lady."

Sarah moved to where she could see Charlotte's face. "Is there anything I can do, beloved? I can send Nate away if you need me." Usually, Charlotte wanted nothing more than to be left alone with a hot brick, a few drops of laudanum, and a darkened room.

Yes, there she was, shaking her head and wincing at the pain. "Go have your reunion, dearest. Love you."

Clarke was at her elbow again. "I'll look after her, my lady." She cast a glance back towards the sitting room door. "You go to your husband."

With a last glance at her poor sister, she did as she was told. Charlotte was a martyr to the woman's trouble; had been ever since that terrible infection after the incident they never spoke about. Fortunately, her courses were not frequent or regular, and the symptoms became bearable again after a day or two.

Furthermore, Sarah usually left her to the tender ministrations of Clarke, who was, after all, with her all the time. It was foolish to feel guilty about welcoming Nate to her bed when Charlotte was in pain and miserable, and would never know the joy and pleasure of being one flesh with a husband.

Well, and are you going to spoil your life—and that of your son and husband—because you cannot improve mine? That's what Charlotte would say if Sarah expressed such thoughts to her. She never complained. Indeed, she compared herself to those whom Sarah rescued, and insisted she had a wonderful and privileged life: wealthy, independent, and surrounded by family who loved her.

"Is she very ill?" Nate asked. She had drifted to where he stood by the sideboard, his bag of clothes still slung over one shoulder. He put down his glass of brandy to brush his fingers across the furrows between her brows. "Does she need you? Do not feel you have to—"

Sarah slipped her arms around his waist and rested her face against his waistcoat. "She has taken something to help her sleep, and her maid is with her. Hold me for a moment, Nate."

He had wrapped her in his embrace even before she had asked. "Gladly."

Sarah felt the tension drain from her as they hugged. She was where she belonged. She pulled back and he released her instantly, watching her as if for a cue. She gave it to him. "Pour me a small brandy, too, Nate, then bring the glasses through to my room."

Her own maid waited, her mouth firmly shut but her eyes full of questions.

"Wilson," Sarah said, "my husband Lord Bentham will be joining me tonight. Please fetch my hot water now, and then that will be all for the night. Oh! And you had better knock before you bring the water in. I am sure, Wilson, I do not need to tell you and Clarke: not a word to the other servants."

Wilson nodded, her eyes wider than ever. "Shall I undo your buttons, Lady Sarah—Lady Bentham, I mean?"

Nate reached Sarah's side, and handed her a glass. "Thank you, Wilson, but I shall be maid for my wife tonight." He kissed Sarah's forehead, and Wilson blinked several times before bobbing a curtsey and stammering, "Yes, my lord. My lady. Um." She bobbed again. "Every happiness. Hot water. Yes." And still bobbing, she hurried from the room, closing the door behind her.

"Poor Wilson. I am afraid she might burst of curiosity."

Nate ran his finger down her cheek and then slid a hand down her arm and across onto her breast, driving what she had been about to say completely out of her head.

His voice was husky as he commented, "She should knock before she comes in, should she?"

Sarah sipped her brandy, trying to pretend she was not going up in flames. "I hoped that was a good idea," she told him.

He sipped his own before answering, his hand continuing its explorations, shaping her breast and then moving to the other. "An excellent idea. But I think I should not strip you naked quite yet?"

She could feel the heat rising in her cheeks. He was bold, this older, more confident Nate. "Nor I, you." She managed the retort, and her voice barely shook.

"Perhaps a kiss, then?" he asked. His hand slid around her back to hold her firm against him, and his lips descended on hers.

For seven years, memories of their kisses and embraces had fuelled her dreams. Tender at first, almost tentative, this kiss set those memories in the shade from the first, and as the heat rose and his free hand pressed her closer; as she spiralled into a space out of time and place where nothing existed but him, the memories slipped away to be replaced by new ones.

Somehow, the glasses were gone, and both of his hands were on her, and hers on him, untying and stripping off his cravat, fumbling undone the buttons of his waistcoat, pulling his shirt from his pantaloons so she could slide her hands up under it, to stroke and caress his warm firm skin, silk over steel, much more of it than back when he had been a skinny youth just shooting up from boyhood and still inches short of his adult height.

Such random thoughts surfaced and drifted away as he released her for long enough to wriggle out of his waistcoat, pull the shirt over his head, all the while kissing her as if the touch of her lips were keeping him alive.

Then his hands were on her again, and he was kissing her neck and then lower. With her bodice now completely unfastened, her gown slipped down her body to pool around her feet, and she kicked free of it and curved her spine so he had room to continue to feast while she pressed the rest of her body to his.

The knock on the door was repeated twice before either of them surfaced enough to notice.

She left his arms reluctantly, and picked up a robe on the way to the door. "It will be Wilson with the hot water."

He caught her arm; just a touch, but it was enough to stop her. "Will she be more likely to talk to the other servants about us if she knows the truth? Or if she doesn't?"

Sarah shook her head. "Wilson will not talk. Not when I have asked her not to do so. But still..."

The knock sounded again, and Sarah opened the door, wide enough that Wilson could carry in the large jug of water. The maid's eyes fixed on Nate's naked torso and widened so far, the white showed all around the iris.

"I will just put this on the washstand, my lady. My lord."

"Before you, go, Wilson, my husband and I wish to speak to you."

Wilson slopped the water as she put the jug down. "I did not tell anyone, my lady. I will not."

Sarah nodded. "I know. You have been a loyal servant to me these past two years, since the duke insisted that he could afford to give me and Charlotte a maid each. When I go to live with my husband, I shall still need a maid who is used to my ways and whom I know I can trust. Will you come with me, Wilson?"

"I am heir to an earl, if that helps," Nate offered.

"I know, my lord. That is, the servants know you have been paying court to my lady. No one knows that you have wed her."

"Seven years ago," Sarah told her. "We were wed seven years ago, Wilson, and then torn apart by my father and grandfather, who sent Nate far away and told me our marriage was a lie. But now he is back and we are together again."

It was the right note to take with a woman who loved horrid novels. Her eyes shone, and she pressed her hands together under her chin. "It is just like a story!" she breathed out.

"We need to tell Elias before we tell anyone else," Sarah added. "Keep our secret, even within the house, until tomorrow afternoon, Wilson. After that, we will begin to let others know, and at the end of the week, His Grace plans to announce it to the whole of Society at a ball."

"Ooooh!" Wilson was clearly thrilled to her core. "It is just like *The Lost Little Lord*. He is your son, then, my lady, and yours, my lord. The legitimate heir, stolen from his people and labouring in poverty! You can trust me, my lady. I will not say a word until you give me leave. Oh, the dear little boy!"

Dismissed, she floated from the room with a dreamy smile.

Nate chuckled. "I hope you plan for us to speak to Elias soon, my love, before your maid bursts." He took her back into his arms and bent to kiss her ear and then behind it and down her throat.

Sarah, as she felt her robe slipping to the floor, retained enough sense to answer, "In the morning, Nate. We will go up to the nursery in the morning."

15

Half an hour later, Sarah lay in Nate's arms, her head pillowed on his shoulder. His mind, which had stopped working somewhere between their kiss by the door and the moment they tumbled naked into the bed, had begun turning over again, even though most of it was still occupied with vague thoughts best summed up in the Scots word 'Wow!'

He dropped a kiss onto her hair. "I love you," he said, again. He had lost count of the number of repetitions this evening alone. But it was worth saying again.

"I love you, too," she replied, and shifted so that she could meet his eyes. "I do not remember it being so good, Nate. Can we do it again?"

"Soon," he assured her, and even the question had his masculine equipment stirring with interest. "I was not patient," he added. "Next time, let me see if I can do better. Seven years is a long time to be celibate."

Her eyebrows lifted. "Were you? All the time? I thought you were a sailor—do they not say a girl in every port?"

A rather clumsy interrogation, but she had the right to know, after all. "I cannot claim an excess of virtue, dearest heart. I thought

I had lost you forever, that you had been forced to marry someone else. But my only experience was with you, and that was sublime. I could not bear the thought of lying with any other woman. And the mere idea of being one in a line of men, with a female anxious to get it over, take my coin, and move to the next encounter… It shrivelled me where I stood. But when I refused the services offered from the comfort boats, the other sailors took exception." He smiled at the memory of his solution.

"So, I took the whore of my choice off to a private corner where we wouldn't be observed, told her I was wed and didn't plan to break my vows, and paid her to keep silent about what we did. She took my money and went to sleep."

She and later co-conspirators must have spoken among their colleagues, because whenever the ship returned to a port they'd been before, the pleasure girls would fight among themselves for the chance to be the one to go off with him. In time he was appointed the doctor's assistant and also grew tall and broad enough to hold his own in a fight, and he was able to give up the masquerade.

Sarah kissed his chin. "Clever. I would not have... That is, I would have forgiven you if..."

Nate kissed her back, and no nonsense with chins, either. When she surfaced for air, he told her, "I kept my vows, Sarah, my love. I will not say I was not tempted from time to time, for I am only a man. But all my dreams have been of you, and I have never danced the horizontal hornpipe with anyone else."

The piece of navy slang had her giggling, but she replied, "Nor I. You know I planned to find a husband, but it was for Elias, and every man I put on my list got crossed off again."

Nate, well into his second wind, was losing interest in the conversation. "In fairness, I should tell you that, when the woman I was with was not tired, we talked about a woman's pleasure. I know I was ignorant in the beginning, my love. I set out to learn how to bring my future wife—who always had your face, my love—the same joy you gave me, and who better to learn from than a woman whose business is pleasure?"

His hands were between them now, seeking to find what made

her gasp; what made her moan, and it was on a moan that she said, "You were a good student, then, beloved."

Their conjugal activities in the three days of their marriage had been pleasant, much better than the awkwardness of the first time. Pleasant was a totally inadequate word for what Sarah had experienced the previous night. Twice.

Again, this morning, when they first woke, and nearly a fourth time when they were assisting each other to dress, except that Wilson had knocked on the door with her hot chocolate, and with a choice of beverages for Nate.

As Sarah sat before her mirror while Wilson pinned her hair up into a simple roll, her eyes kept drifting to where Nate leaned against a post of the bed, sipping his morning coffee, composed and handsome in fawn pantaloons and a waistcoat in a rich dark red over his snowy shirt. She had set the silver pin in his cravat, and been rewarded with a kiss that made it necessary to tie the cravat again.

Every time their eyes met, he smiled, and his smile sent a warm thrill right to her core. She had wondered if his casual touches, his burning glances, would have less power after they had been intimate again, but the opposite appeared to be true.

She took a deep breath to compose herself. They had sent a message down to the kitchens and up to the nursery to let them know that two more adults would be joining Elias for breakfast. "Thank you, Wilson. That looks very nice," she told the maid.

"Beautiful," Nate agreed. "But you have good material to work with, Wilson."

The maid blushed and agreed. "Yes, my lord. I'll just tidy up here, my lady, shall I?"

"Thank you, Wilson," Sarah said again. She caught up the shawl she had ready. The passages of the great house could be chilly at this time of the year. Nate shrugged into his coat, which closely fitted his broad shoulders and chest, but not so tightly he needed assistance to take it on and off. Though she had helped him with his evening jacket last night, and blushed at the thought.

"What lovely thoughts prompt that delicious colour?" he whispered in her ear, as they left the room arm in arm.

"I suspect I shall spend much of my life blushing at my thoughts," she retorted. "You are a bad influence on me, Nate." She leaned into him, bumping his shoulder with hers.

"A lifelong ambition fulfilled," he teased, making her giggle.

She stopped to check on Charlotte. She was as white as bone, and tense with the stillness that hinted at feared pain if she moved. However, she insisted she was comfortable, and would be able to get up later. "You must both visit me, and tell me how Elias has taken the news," she insisted. "Now smile, darling. You know I am like this when my inconvenience is on me, and I shall be well directly."

Sarah had to smile as she acknowledged the truth of that.

Nate was waiting in the sitting room. She would never tire of seeing his eyes light up as she came towards him. "How is your sister, my love?"

"Uncomfortable," she admitted, "but she will be better tomorrow, or the next day." She could not resist leaning in to kiss him. "She is happy for us. Let us go and have breakfast with our son."

The footman stationed on this wing kept his eyes firmly fixed on the painting opposite him as Sarah and Nate passed. Sarah, who had been leaning on Nate's arm, straightened, but the joy kept bubbling up in a smile.

The secondary staircase at the end of the wing was deserted, and they soon let themselves into the main passage that ran through the nursery and schoolroom floor. Sarah sobered at the thought of the explanation to come. She and Nate had discussed it the night before and again this morning.

They would be honest with Elias from the beginning. They owed him that. But what would he think?

A footman opened the door into the complex of rooms that formed the nursery. The door opened directly into the day nursery, and Elias, his face painfully clean and beaming with delight, was there to greet them.

"Mama!" And then, with a glance at his nurse, "Good morning, Mama." He bowed to Nate, grinning. "Good morning, Lord Bentham. How are your sisters this morning?"

"They were well when I saw them yesterday, Elias," Nate told him, while Sarah fought the panic that threatened to close her throat. She masked her anxiety by sweeping forward to sink to her knees and give her son a hug and kiss on the cheek.

"Now?" Nate asked. Sarah nodded. Best to get it done before she ran screaming from the room.

"Elias, come and sit by the window. There is something your mother and I wish to tell you."

Elias obediently took a seat, and Sarah sat beside him, taking his warm hand in her cold one. Nate squatted on his heels before them. They had agreed that Nate would start the story, and Sarah would add what she felt was needed.

Before he could speak, Elias said, "She is not truly my mother, sir. But I love her just as if she were."

Sarah could not quite account for the tears in her eyes. Regret at the lies her dear son had lived with? Fear of his reaction? Joy at the life before them? Perhaps all of these.

Nate replied to the boy. "I would like to tell you about your true mother and father, Elias, if you would like to hear."

Elias stiffened and went still, his eyes huge in his face. He nodded, a single jerk of his head.

Nate settled back onto the carpet, his legs crossed at the ankles, his elbows on his knees. The position put him below Elias, so he was looking up into the boy's anxious face. "First, I should say that Lady Sarah knew some of this, and I knew some, but neither of us knew the whole until we shared what we knew with one another."

Elias gave another jerky nod.

"Your mother was very young when she became acquainted with your father. Just fifteen, and as lovely as a fairy princess. They had seen one another before, when she stayed in the house her father owned near the village where he lived. But her grandfather owned many houses, and this was not a favourite of his. They didn't come often or stay for long. Until that summer."

"Was her grandfather rich?" Elias asked.

"Very. And important. He was friends with the King and a leader in the House of Lords. Her father was his heir. Your father was not important at all, or rich. He was seventeen, your father. His father was the local vicar, and your father was his father's steward and errand boy and groom. So your mother was as far out of his reach as the stars in the sky."

Sarah took up the tale, unable to resist. "She was lonely, and had nothing to do. She and her sister had been very ill, and they had been sent to the country to rest and recover. When your mother was well again, your aunt still spent most of her days sleeping. Your mother started to wander the woods and the fields near their house."

They continued that way, taking it in turns, telling of Nate's approach to Sarah's father, of his exile, of his plan and their elopement, their marriage.

Elias listened without comment until they got to Nate's beating and abduction, and subsequent career in the navy. "Why didn't he come back? Didn't he want me?"

"He didn't know about you, Elias." Nate told him. "He should have come back for his wife, once he could. But it was three years more before he had rank enough for the navy to listen him, and by then he thought her grandfather would have made her marry someone else. He thought coming back would make trouble for her."

Elias turned his attention to Sarah. Had he guessed what they were about, or was it just it was her turn to tell a part of the story. "Didn't my mother want me?"

"Very much. When she knew you were coming, she was frightened of what her grandfather might do, but she was very happy to think she would have you to love. You were taken from her when you were born." The tears that had been threatening throughout the recital overflowed. "They wouldn't even let me hold you. I spent years trying to find you. I thought about you every day."

"You?" Elias's voice was hushed and strained. "You are my true mama?" He drew away from her, just a little. She put out her hand, but stopped herself from touching him.

"I am your true mama. I was so happy when Mrs Wakefield found you for me, Elias."

"You did not tell me." It was a cry of sorrow, flavoured with a world of betrayal.

"Elias," Nate said it again, when Elias didn't shift his disappointed eyes away from Sarah. "Elias." This time, the boy turned to him. "Elias, your mama told me what they said to you at the house party; what they said at the workhouse."

No answer, but Nate continued, "She did not know I was alive, believed what her grandfather told her, that we were not truly married. She would have told you the truth when you were older; when she could be sure you would not accidentally speak of it to someone who would use the knowledge to say things that hurt. Someone who tried to make you ashamed of who you are. Do you understand what I mean?"

Elias thought about that and his body softened until he was leaning against Sarah, and her arms were around him. "I suppose so. That old grandfather was a bad, bad man."

"He was," Nate agreed.

"When did you find out that Mama had me?" Elias demanded, but he did not try to leave Sarah's embrace.

"Two days ago," Nate told him. "Someone had mentioned a ward, but it wasn't until I heard how old you were that I guessed."

Again, those accusing eyes. "Why did you not tell him, Mama?"

And once more, Nate answered for her. "Your mama and I had not seen one another for seven years. She needed to know I was still a man who could love you and her, and be kind to you both. She could not trust your safety to just anyone."

Elias relaxed again, thinking that over, while Sarah used the handkerchief that Nate passed her to mop her eyes. After a while, the boy spoke again, his shy smile at last in evidence. "Is Norie my cousin, then, Father?"

At the form of address, Nate's eyes filled, and he had to clear his throat before he could reply. "She and her sisters are my half-sisters, my son, so they are your aunts."

Elias sat up straight at that, his eyebrows shooting up. "My aunts? That is ridiculous." He shook his head. "One of them is just a baby. Can we go and visit my aunts, Mama?"

Sarah looked a question at Nate, who answered, "I will send a message to my stepmama, Lady Lechton, and ask when would be convenient, Elias. I know both she and my father, your grandfather, are anxious to meet you."

The revelation to Elias had gone better than Nate expected. Over breakfast, he answered question after question about his family, his life in the navy and his work as a doctor. Elias said nothing about the future, but surely he must wonder?

Nate introduced the topic. "Your mother and I have not yet talked about where the three of us will live now that we've found one another again," he said.

The flare of hope in Elias's eyes was unmistakable. "I am to come with you?" he asked.

"You are our son. The three of us belong together," Sarah told him.

"We have been robbed of so many years," Nate added. "I want you and I want your mother. I want us to be a family." Sarah nodded and so did Elias, and when it was time to leave Elias to his lessons, he gave Sarah a hug, hesitated, then stepped into Nate's welcoming arm, for a hug that turned into a friendly wrestle.

Sarah took the moment to speak to the nursemaid. Nate didn't think Elias, currently consumed with giggles, was listening, but he heard Sarah tell the maid to feel free to discuss the story she'd heard with the other servants. "We will not be announcing our marriage until the ball at the end of the week, but after that, we want to spread the news of our marriage and of Elias's parentage as far and as quickly as possible," she said.

"Poor Morris," she commented to Nate as they left. "Elias is going to have trouble focusing this morning, and who can blame him?"

"Who, indeed? I feel that way myself," Nate said.

He continued on down the stairs while Sarah went to check on her sister. He found Lord Andrew in the breakfast room, finishing his breakfast while reading the morning paper. "My father is in his study, Bentham. He wishes to talk to you about settlements."

"Will you let Sarah know where I've gone?" Nate asked.

The duke had a hot pot of coffee waiting for him to drink, and a draft marriage settlement for him to read. "This is a close copy of the one we prepared for my daughter Ruth, Bentham. Or can I call you Nathaniel?"

"Nate, Your Grace, if it pleases you."

"Nate, then, and I am Uncle James to my nieces, and to you, if you will. Read it through, Nate, and let me know if you have any concerns."

He began to read through the first sheet of the neatly written stack of pages. "Has Sarah read this, sir?"

"You wish her to do so?" the duke asked.

James looked up to see the man smiling. "I do, Your Gr–Uncle James." He had better get used to the familiar form of address. "She will have an opinion, I am sure."

"Good man," Uncle James replied. "My niece is an independent young woman, and I am pleased you realise that."

"You should know that I am not in need of her dowry, sir. My inheritance from my mother's father was invested during my minority, and I have added to it the prize money I received over the years. I have an independent income that will keep her and Elias, and any further children we have, in comfort until I inherit my father's estate, which is substantial."

Uncle James raised his eyebrows. "Indeed? I understood from your father that you were dependent on an allowance. He told me that he would reinstate it even though you went against his wishes, since your rebellion has resulted in a grandson."

Nate grinned. "My father's threats to remove my allowance

would be more effective if he had ever actually paid me one. He has not, and I do not need it."

"I see." The duke sat back to sip his coffee, and Nate continued reading the settlement papers, which seemed very fair.

He was interrupted when a knock on the door heralded Sarah. She wore a bonnet and pelisse over a walking dress, and was drawing gloves onto her hands.

"Darling," he said, "you are in time to help me argue marriage settlements with your uncle."

Sarah smiled, but replied, "I would like to look at them later, but may I leave you to it, Nate? Uncle James? Charlotte has had a message from one of the businesses that gives employment to her school pupils. There is a question of theft, apparently. The proprietor is insisting on seeing Charlotte immediately, or she will be calling the constables."

Uncle James nodded. "Charlotte has asked you to go in her place?"

"No. She was trying to get dressed to go herself. She is certain it must be a mistake. I told her to behave, and I would do the errand for her."

"May I escort you?" Nate asked, taking her hand.

"You finish what you are doing," Sarah insisted. "I have a coachman, a footman and my guard, and I should not be above an hour." She reached up and kissed his cheek. "Send that message to your father, Nate. I will be back in plenty of time to take Elias to meet him this afternoon."

16

Maggie Wilton ran a stable of seamstresses and embroiderers out of an attic five floors up in a rickety building on an obscure little alley in Clerkenwell. The coachman had to stop in the broader street beyond the alley, and he stayed nervously with the horses, his musket over his knees.

Yahzak argued that he should run the errand on his own; that the lady should not be going into such a narrow space. "I will fetch the girl, and this Wilton woman will not stop me," he assured her. John, the footman, nodded. "Or I could go, my lady."

Sarah was very tempted to take them up on the offer. She wanted the errand over and done so she could return to Nate. But she had promised Charlotte to see to it. "If the constables are already there, they will listen to a duke's niece, but not to either of you. And you will keep me safe." It was a poor street, but not an impossible one. The houses were rundown and ramshackle, but the front steps and windows were clean, and no more rubbish littered the corners than might collect in a day or two.

"It is one woman and a dozen girls, Yahzak Bey," Sarah pointed out.

"I go first," he decreed. "If I see anything suspicious, we return to the carriage."

He led the way, one hand inside his coat where his pistol hid, and the other on the knife in his pocket.

Sarah followed, and John brought up the rear.

The building was typical for the area—a shop on the ground floor, a street door to the side of it onto a stairway that led up to flats above. Sarah glanced back, but the carriage was out of sight. The stairwell smelt of cabbage, but not of the worse things Sarah sometimes encountered on her rescue visits.

The stairs turned tightly, with two flights for each storey and a door opening into a flat on every second landing. They climbed past the sounds of children crying, then of a woman singing in a foreign language, and then of a man and woman arguing.

On the next floor, with only two flights to go to the top, the door was partly open but all was silent within. Yahzak paused and gave the door a suspicious glare, then continued up the stairs, peering ahead. "I hear talking," he reported.

Sarah could, too: the hum of female voices coming from the attic above. She turned the corner to the final flight of stairs, speeding her climb so close to her goal.

She was on Yahzak's heels when he knocked on the open door and stepped into the room beyond. When he dropped like a stone, the man who had hit him was able to reach through and drag her, struggling and shouting, into the attic. She tried to get her hand into her reticule, but dropped it in the struggle. A dozen young girls sat on low chairs, fabric over their laps, their needles poised in the air, their eyes wide, and their mouths open.

Sarah screamed her fear and anger. The man who held her jerked the arm around her throat. "Shut up, bitch, or I'll break your neck."

Yahzak lay just inside the door, the club his assailant had used to fell him beside him. She could not tell whether he still lived. Beyond him, a thin-faced woman with narrow eyes and a sour expression watched the scene as if it were a play, and not an entertaining one.

"You are making a mistake," Sarah said. The man jerked her

head back, a brutal warning. Behind him, the clump of boots heralded the arrival of more men. At least two, perhaps three. Not John, who was wearing shoes. John must have been assaulted, too.

"Gag her and bind her," her captor ordered, and another bulky brute moved into view to shove a cloth into the mouth her captor forced open. It tasted foul, and she tried to spit it out, but he was tying it in place with another cloth around her head. Her fear receded at the indication she was not immediately to be killed, or perhaps it was just swamped by her rising anger.

While all eyes were on her head, she kicked the reticule, and the pistol it contained, so it slid across the room to the row of seamstresses. One of them quickly covered it with her skirt. Perhaps they would be able to use it to save John and Yahzak.

The man who held her tied her hands together, and then her feet, before hoisting her over his shoulder. She caught a glimpse of two other men, also hard brutes. Four men to take out her and her escort. It was, of course, a trap, but what for? Ransom?

The thin-faced woman spoke for the first time. "Here, what about the man? You can't leave him here. If he wakes up, he'll tell them I gave her to you."

"Your problem," the first man said.

"There's another one on the stairs." That was one of the other men.

"Her problem," the first man repeated. "We've got a delivery to make." He glared at the silent seamstresses. "Keep your mouths shut or I'll come back and kill the lot of you."

The thin-faced woman followed them down to the flat on the floor below, wringing her hands and complaining. John lay unconscious just inside the door. Two of them stuffed Sarah into a large sack, ignoring John and the complaining woman as well. Through the stink of the gag, Sarah could smell wheat.

"You can't leave 'im 'ere in my flat," the woman shrieked, but Sarah's kidnappers didn't reply. Sarah was hoisted back onto a shoulder, and carried downstairs. Her carrier's shoulder dug into her belly, and he bumped her head on a wall or doorway a couple of times as he turned corners. She tried to ignore the pain, block out the panic, and listen for any clue about what was happening.

Now they were outside. Perhaps her driver would see them, but no. All he would see was a man carrying a sack. In any case, as far as she could tell, they had turned the other way in the alley. Fifty paces, more or less, and she was dumped onto wood. A cart. She could hear someone clicking his tongue and telling a horse to gee up, and then she was being jostled around against the moving surface.

They drove for what seemed a long time. She couldn't tell if all her kidnappers were still with her, because they didn't speak; the only voices she heard were the driver's occasional command to the horses, and people farther away, talking in the streets as they passed.

They wanted her, or rather Charlotte, alive. She kept reminding herself of that, shying away from the question of what they would do when they found they had the wrong twin. If they found out. She wasn't going to tell them. Not unless it gave her an advantage.

At last, the cart stopped and someone hoisted her back onto a shoulder. She felt the change in the air, heard the difference in the footsteps, as they entered a building. "Got her," someone said. The first man, she thought.

"Bring her through here." That was a woman's voice, and one of some refinement, though with a hint of the slums in some of the vowels.

Sarah was dropped to the floor with a thud. "Careful! Don't bruise the merchandise!" the woman growled.

Merchandise? That couldn't be good. The sack was opened, shaken, so that she slid out, feet first, and landed in a heap on the carpet in a small parlour. Sarah's first impression was of gilt, red velvet, and too many mirrors. Her second was of cut-price workmanship.

She sat up and looked at the woman who had presumably ordered her kidnapping: a plump female in her middle years, heavily painted and in a dress that matched the room—gaudy and cheaply made.

The woman glared at her as one of the brutes fumbled at the knot of her gag. "You are not Lady Charlotte Winderfield," the woman said. "Charley, this is not Charlotte Winderfield. This is her sister, Lady Sarah."

The man addressed as Charley looked at Sarah as if it were her fault. "Maybe the gent won't mind," he suggested. "One skirt is much like another. Still a lady, isn't she?"

The woman narrowed her eyes at Sarah in speculation. "Maybe. But it was Lady Charlotte we paid that silly bint Wilton for, and Lady Charlotte the gentleman ordered. What were you doing there, Lady Sarah?"

Sarah spat out the disgusting lump of sodden cloth. "Lady Bentham," she said. It sounded ridiculous, insisting on her married name, but perhaps the fact she was a Viscountess and the daughter-in-law of an earl would add weight to her status as a duke's niece and convince these idiots to let her go. If, as she supposed, a gentleman had hoped to pressure Charlotte into marrying him, the fact that she was here instead, and was married, would put a spoke in his wheel.

"Oo's Lady Bentham?" Charley asked.

"I am. I am married to Viscount Bentham, heir to the Earl of Lechton. Your men kidnapped me while I was running a message for my sister."

The woman cursed long and fluently. Sarah understood about half the words and all of the tone. When the woman ran down, she said to Charley, "'E won't want her now. Get rid of 'er." She had lost her imitation of genteel speech in her agitation.

"Send 'er back, you mean?" Charley asked.

The woman sneered. "Kill her, fat wit. She has seen me and you. We'll hang if she gets free and she's no use to 'im married."

"Seems a waste of a choice bit of skirt. We could put 'er to work in the 'ouse," Charley suggested.

"And risk 'er escaping? I wouldn't 'ave touched 'er, even when the Beast set it all up, if the gentleman 'adn't been prepared to pay two thousand gold, and take 'er out of the country. If he don't want 'er, we 'ave to get rid of 'er before 'er family comes looking."

Charley nodded, slowly, but one of the other men cleared his throat. "Shouldn't we ask the gennelman? 'E could make 'er a widow easy enough. And there's 'arf the fee still to come."

Sarah saw the woman consider this suggestion and was relieved at the thoughtful nod. "Very well. Lock her upstairs, and I'll get a message to him."

17

Nate held on as Aldridge raced his phaeton towards the address Lady Charlotte had given them, weaving close to buildings, feathering past carriages, missing pedestrians by inches, turning corners on a single wheel.

Nate, Drew, and the duke had been about to go upstairs to the nursery when Aldridge arrived, asking anxiously for Charlotte. He had word of a trap set in Clerkenwell—someone who planned to compromise and marry Sarah's sister. What would the kidnappers do when they found out they had the wrong sister, and a married woman, at that?

It might all be a lie. The informant was Lord Ashbury's sister-in-law, the former Lady Ashbury. Her betrayals were multiple. Whether she was now betraying the slum king who was her brother or still working for him remained to be seen. If she was telling the truth, they had no time to lose.

If they arrived in time, it would be thanks to Aldridge's driving skill. On any other day, Nate would be demanding that he slow down, take care. But with Sarah in trouble, he just gripped the side rail of the seat and gritted his teeth, and prayed as he had never prayed before.

How would he tell Elias if anything had happened to her? How would he survive losing her again?

Aldridge hauled the horses to a halt beside a carriage with the Winshire coat of arms. "You're Lady Sarah's driver?" he asked the man who sat nervously atop the carriage, a musket across his knees.

"Aye, sir." The coachman looked towards a narrow gap between the buildings. "I'm waiting for Lady Bentham."

Nate leapt to the ground, the pistol Uncle James had given him in one hand and his dagger in the other. "How long since my wife went in there, driver?"

"Perhaps fifteen minutes, sir?" the driver answered. "Is there something wrong?"

Aldridge shouted at a man who was lounging against a wall. "You there?!" The man spat a stream of yellow coloured bile into the street and sneered. A coin appeared between Aldridge's fingers and disappeared as quickly.

"I am the Marquis of Aldridge and I am giving you two options. You make sure no one touches my carriage or my horses or those of Lady Bentham, and you get a crown. Anything happens to either team or rig, and I find you and extract your brains through your nostrils, burn them, and sell them as pie filling. Your choice." He held up the coin. "A shilling now, the rest when I come back."

The man straightened. "Done." He held out a hand and caught the coin that Aldridge tossed even as Nate ran past him into the alley.

"Stay here and tell the duke where we've gone," he heard Aldridge tell the driver before following after him, catching up as Nate reached the narrow stairs that led to the attic that they'd been told had been used to lay a trap for Charlotte.

They heard the arguing from above before they began the steep climb. A shrill female voice was demanding that a problem be removed, while at least two males were arguing that killing the servants of a duke was only going to make things worse.

It was enough to warn them to make their approach quiet. The combatants were so intent on their dispute that Nate and Aldridge were able to get all the way to the fourth floor, where a scrawny female and two men—one tall and skinny, and the other short and bulky, stood over the tied-up body of a man in Winshire livery, arguing about whether to kill him, let him go, or dump him still living into the Thames.

The bonnet on the woman's head ratcheted Nate's wrath several more notches. He had last seen it on Sarah.

He had time to wonder whether the ducal scion would be any good in a fight—no polite gentlemanly rules here—before the short man looked up and saw them reach the landing, Nate still a little in the lead.

At his gasp, the other two turned, but by then Nate and Aldridge were upon them. Nate had learned his combat skills in a dirty school, fighting the French, pirates and privateers for His Majesty's Royal Navy, and any number of scoundrels in ports around the world who thought an English sailor might be good for a coin or two.

He took the short man, hurling all his weight at him to take him down, and keeping him there with a knife to the throat. He didn't know where Aldridge learned to fight, but the marquis had the tall man subdued in seconds, with a punch to his gut followed by a knee to his crotch and an elbow to his chin as he curled over his injured jewels.

The woman abandoned her colleagues to run away down the stairs, straight into the arms of the duke and his men. In moments, the three miscreants were bound. Drew knelt by the footman, removing his gag and cutting through his ropes.

"I'm sorry, Your Grace. Someone jumped me from behind. Her ladyship? And Mr Yahzak?"

The duke put a hand on his man's shoulder. "We'll find them, John. We'll check upstairs." As he spoke, a yell came from upstairs. "Kagan!"

Nate, with his wife's bonnet in one hand, led the way again, up into the space under the sloping roof, where a row of high windows gave light to the group of girls who sat with fabric on their laps, their hands still, their eyes wide and fearful.

One of them had crept from her seat and was trying to use her scissors to saw through the ropes that tied the duke's guardsman, who let out a burst of foreign words as the duke and then Drew entered behind Nate.

Drew turned to translate for Nate and Aldridge. "Yahzak was knocked out as well, and the girls know nothing; only that their mistress had four men waiting for Sarah, and that they took her, not ten minutes ago."

"We shall question their mistress," the duke said. "Young women, I appreciate your help to my liege man, here. Your mistress will not be returning. If you need work or shelter, you may depend upon me. But right now, I need to rescue my niece."

One of the girls curtseyed and held out a pretty reticule. "She dropped this, sir." Nate took several steps into the room to take it. He felt the gun inside. Damn.

They cut the bindings on Sarah's ankles and then two of them hustled her upstairs. She stumbled across the room they pushed her into, and stood by the bed, glaring at them.

One of them grinned, showing his gums and a few crooked teeth. He started towards her with his hands out, but the other grabbed him by his collar and jerked him back. "Leave 'er alone."

"I just want to squeeze 'er titties and maybe 'ave a feel," the would-be assailant whined.

"And 'ave 'Is Grace slice out yer gizzard if'n 'e decides to keep 'er? 'E'll fillet ye like a fish if'n ye touch what's 'is."

The lascivious light went out of Three Tooth. "Maybe 'e won't want 'er. Not the right one, 'er downstairs says."

"If'n 'e doesn't, we can all take turns afore we kill 'er, but for now, leave 'er alone." The other dragged Three Tooth towards the door.

"We should tie 'er to the bed," Three Tooth suggested.

The other looked past him to where Sarah still stood, as straight as she could manage, trying to make sure her face did not show fear, disgust, and her dawning hope. *Let them go away and leave me loose*, she prayed.

"Let her alone, you idiot. What's she goin' to do, a fine lady like that? Climb out through the bars with 'er 'ands tied?"

The door shut behind them, and Sarah let out a sigh of relief. He was right about the bars. They only rose halfway up the tall sash windows, but high enough to keep a bound person contained. Apart from that, the small room contained a bedframe with a bare mattress that stank of sweat and sex, a washstand with no bowl, jug, or chamber pot, and nothing else.

No sheets. No drapes. Nothing to hang from the bars to assist her escape.

First things first. Sarah sat on the floor and pulled up her hems so that she could reach the knife that she had begun carrying in a boot sheath ever since Ruth was abducted last year.

After several attempts, she gave up on trying to turn it against the bindings at her wrists. She couldn't both hold the knife and use it. She pulled her hems higher and squeezed the handle between her knees, but the first brush of the blade to her bindings pushed the knife flat.

Tears rose, but she forced them back. Crying wouldn't help her get home to Elias and Nate. How long would it be before he and Uncle James missed her? Before they came looking and found her trail? She did not doubt that they would, but every minute they were delayed made it more likely that Yahzak's and John's lives would be forfeit; that this mysterious gentleman would either order her killed or spirit her away.

His grace, one of the brutes had said. What duke was in need of a bride, and was immoral enough to steal one? Only one man qualified, and he had applied to Uncle James for Charlotte's hand some months ago. Charlotte had, of course, refused him. Even in a society that forgave wealthy titled men almost everything, the Duke of Richport was beyond the pale. But time enough to think about that later.

Inspiration struck. She held the knife above her head with her bound hands and slammed it down into the wooden floor. More by luck than good management, she'd thrust it in between two floor boards, and she leaned on it now, forcing all her weight onto the top of the handle to wedge it securely.

Almost four inches of blade still protruded from the floor. Carefully, doing her best to keep her flesh away from the knife, she began to rub the rope against the sharpened edge.

Several times in the drawn-out minutes that followed, she heard footsteps approaching, and swung away, sitting almost on the knife to hide it from the door. Twice, whoever it was continued on down the passage. The third time, she almost didn't stop sawing at the rope, but it was as well she changed her mind, for she heard a rattle in the lock, the door opened, and the man they called Charley brought in a small loaf of bread and a jug of water.

He laughed to see her sitting there. "Too fine for the bed, are ye, princess?"

"It smells," she told him.

He laughed even harder as he put the jug down on the washstand, and dropped the bread on the floor. "Missus said to give ye some food and drink. Didn't say ye 'ad to 'ave it on a plate."

Still laughing, he left, and she heard the key turn again.

She knelt once more, and inspected the rope. It had been knotted several times, but if she could just get through the last few strands still holding before the main knot, she could pull the rest loose enough to wriggle her hands out.

A few more minutes of sawing, and a sting that had her biting back a whimper when her hands slipped and got sliced. *There!* She pulled and twisted, and the blood from her cut spread across the rope and dripped onto her skirt, but one hand, and then the other, was free.

She inspected the cut, wiping it with a strip torn from her petticoat and then binding the strip as best she could one-handed. The wound was shallow and of no moment, but the blood might get in her way.

Now for the window. If she could drop the upper sash, she could easily climb out, but then where would she go? Her sister's protégé Tony had escaped from Wharton by climbing to the roof. From down here on the floor, impeded by the bars from getting a closer look, she could not tell whether that route was open to her.

Another moment's thought, and she removed her petticoat and tore it into more strips. Three of them tied together made a broad band long enough to wrap around her thighs to cross over and tie around her waist, trapping her skirt into a semblance of pantaloons that was neither elegant nor seemly.

But it was practical. She and Charlotte hadn't clambered over every suitable tree within the home woods in every one of the ducal estates across England without learning a little about proper wear for climbing.

The ankle boots had to go. She took them and her stockings off, and used the stockings to tie the boots to the back of her improvised waistband. She'd need them when she reached the street.

With a good grip on the bars, she climbed onto the windowsill, wrinkling her nose at the sticky grimy feel of the dirty wood under her toes. Carefully, she undid the catches that held the upper sash, and pressed her palms against the frame on either side to ease it down, holding her breath and letting it out when the sash slid down quietly.

Climbing up the bars to the open part of the window presented a challenge. She would get partway and then stick until her strength failed and she would slip down again. Fear of never seeing Elias and Nate again kept her trying. She could never afterwards remember how she finally pulled herself up.

Down to the street or up to the roof? Below, several hefty men loitered by the door to the building. Down would get her caught again. Up was her only choice.

After that, the only difficult part was ignoring the drop. A pipe ran close by the window, giving her something to cling to, as she used the ornamental carvings that festooned the building as footholds in her climb. This must have been an important building, in its time, before this part of London sunk into a slum.

She reached the roof and dropped flat for a rest before trying to find a way across the roofs as far as she could get from her captors' lair. A stir below had her peeping over the edge in time to see her rescue arrive—Nate in a phaeton driven by Lord Aldridge, and Uncle James and Drew on horseback with a full dozen of the guard. The bawd's men scattered at their approach, and disappeared in the other direction, or down narrow ways between buildings.

Sarah didn't want to shout. No point in alerting a villain who might reach her before her family did. She felt in her hair and found she had retained a few hairpins. With a handful of them, she began peppering the men who were below, having a conversation before storming the house. Deciding strategy, beyond a doubt.

Two of her pins must have struck, for one of the guards exclaimed and looked up, and then Lord Aldridge. He grinned and grabbed Nate by the arm, saying something and pointing upward.

They were all gazing up, now, but Sarah had her eyes locked on Nate, and he had his on her, his smile a broad beam, his eyes full of warmth.

18

*S**he is safe.** Nate bounded up the stairs of the rooming house next door, having given the landlady such a generous bribe she would probably have sold him half the tenants, and not just access to the roof. The fear and anger that had driven him across London still roiled in his gut, a hollow burning ache.

She is safe, he thought again as he stepped out onto the roof and she walked into his arms, filling the emptiness. "I have never been more frightened in my life," he murmured in her ear.

"I knew you would come to rescue me," she replied, snuggling in as if she wanted him to absorb her, lifting her mouth to his.

He met her lips partway, lingering over a kiss that heated him to the core, transmuting what remained of his distress into a different kind of passion. He caught at the shreds of his self-control and reminded her, "You rescued yourself."

Another kiss. He felt the urgency in her response; understood that it mirrored his own. But a roof in the slums was no place to celebrate her survival, especially when one of the duke's men had followed him up and was leaning over the edge of the roof, signalling to the group below.

"I have a phaeton below. Let us go home." He released her

reluctantly, but took her hand to lead her down the narrow stairs. "Your sister will be beside herself."

"The place next door is a brothel, I think," Sarah told him. "The bawd ordered my kidnap, or Charlotte's rather."

"Yes, the Wilton woman told us." Nate looked back over his shoulder and grinned. "Aldridge has an inventive line in threats and your uncle is plain scary. He and his men are waiting for you to be safely away and for the constables to arrive, and then the bawd and her brawn will be arrested."

"It was an abduction to order. A gentleman, the bawd said. One who wanted to marry Charlotte. One of her bully boys called him 'his grace'. Nate, I think it must be Richport. He made an offer for Charlotte earlier this year."

Nate stopped on one of the landings for another kiss, needing the reassurance of her presence in his arms. "How did they react when they found they had you, instead?"

She shuddered. "Not well. They were waiting to find out if 'the gentleman' would accept me in Charlotte's place. Easy to make me a widow, they said." Her voice broke on the last sentence, and he kissed her again, until the duke's man cleared his throat. He was standing above them on the stair, studiously examining the ceiling.

Nate squeezed his arms around Sarah and released her. "They reckoned without my brave wife. You rescued yourself, and now let us tell your uncle what you've told me, and then I will take you home."

Nate had Sarah's reticule in the phaeton, and she was able to comb her hair and fix it into a simple roll with her remaining hair pins. Enough to keep it under the bonnet that he had also retrieved from Wilton's workshop.

She had replaced her stockings and shoes and tidied her clothes while waiting for Nate. She probably still looked ruffled and untidy, but not enough to draw attention as they crossed town.

Nate lifted her up into the phaeton—Aldridge's, apparently. The marquis and Drew had gone into the brothel to keep the bawd and her men distracted until the arrival of the constables Uncle James had sent for.

She and Nate passed them as they drove away. Two of Uncle James's fierce retainers accompanied a group of perhaps half a dozen, Bow Street Horse Patrol men by their red waistcoats. The guardsmen grinned at Sarah and exchanged acknowledgements with the two guardsmen who had been sent to escort her and Nate back across London.

As they drove, Nate told her how Aldridge had brought the warning, and she asked him about the footman and Yahzak. But most of the trip was taken in silence, Sarah with her hand tucked around Nate's arm, leaning against him to feel his strength and his warmth.

As the streets grew wider and the houses larger and more fash-ionable, she began to see people she knew. Nate kept the phaeton to as fast a pace as possible, while Sarah returned any greetings with nothing more than a wave or a nod, though the nods became harder and harder to manage as her headache built, until it throbbed with every bump in the road, swam with every sway around a corner.

At last, they turned into the mews behind Winshire House. Several grooms rushed for the horses, and Barker, the head groom, appeared on her side of the phaeton himself, ready to help her down. "Thank God you are safe, my lady," he said. She swallowed her nausea, braced against the pain, and smiled at him.

The sentiment was repeated over and over, as she entered the house clinging to Nate's arm. They made their way through a throng of servants to the parlour where, or so Grosvenor the butler said, Charlotte was waiting.

Two men stood as they entered—David Wakefield and another, whom she recognised after a moment, even as Nate started forward with a cry of recognition. "Cousin Arthur!"

Sarah braced herself again, smiling at the room, wondering how long she needed to stay before she could seek her bed.

"You look as if you could do with a cup of tea," Charlotte said, as the two men exchanged delighted greetings, and tried to compress seven years of news into a few exclamations.

"I could murder for a cup of tea," Sarah agreed. She sat beside Charlotte, who was looking pale, but better than this morning. She removed her bonnet and her hair tumbled down. "Oh dear. Perhaps I should go up and make myself tidy."

Nate interrupted his conversation to turn to her. "Darling, what am I thinking! Gentlemen, can we continue this another time? I need to see to my wife. Charlotte, could we put my cousin up in a guest room? Sweetheart, how is your head?

"Your father," she reminded him. "We were going to take Elias to see your father."

"I'll let my father know that we have to postpone, and I'll talk to Elias. You are going up to bed, my love."

Bed sounded wonderful. Gratefully, Sarah let her husband coddle her.

Nate fussed over the scrapes and cuts on Sarah's wrists, the bruises she'd accumulated when she was being manhandled. Wilson had ordered up a hot bath, and he insisted on staying while she undressed so that he could inspect all of her wounds.

Since she was a small girl, Sarah had only ever been unclothed in front of two other people—and that rarely—her maid, when in her bath, and her husband, in the dark and under the sheets on the three nights—four now—she had spent in bed with him. Stripping in front of him in full daylight had her blushing like a young maiden, which she had not been for seven years.

He set her at ease with his manner: crisp and matter-of-fact, focused on checking that her injuries were no worse than she said. He finished by taking her gently in his arms and pressing a tender kiss to her forehead. "Now have a long soak, my love." He stepped back and held out his hand to help her into the water. The scrapes stung as she lowered herself, but once she was immersed, the heat felt wonderful.

Nate knelt beside the tub, so his head was close to hers. "Wilson is bringing you a soothing herbal tea. If you will permit, dearest heart, I shall go up to see Elias. I daresay some of today's doings might have reached the nursery, though I hope his nursemaid will have had enough sense to keep it from him. If not, I will be able to reassure him that you are home and well."

A swift knock at the door was followed by Wilson's entrance, with a tea tray. She could smell some of Cook's delicious drop scones, and suddenly realised that she was hungry.

"Go, of course," she told him. "Tell him I shall be up to see him later."

"After you have had a sleep," Nate told her, firmly. "I shall be back by the time the water cools, and shall dress those cuts, then tuck you into bed. Drink the willow bark tea first, my love, and then the other. Wilson, stay with your mistress and make sure she doesn't go to sleep in her bath."

It had always annoyed Sarah when other people made decisions for her, but she had seen the shadow of Nate's fear still lurking in his eyes. He needed to take care of her. He needed to nag her gently, because he loved her to distraction and had suffered when she was taken. Her hero.

Sarah obediently downed the willow bark concoction, which had mercifully been sweetened with honey. Then she sat back in the bath, her tea in one hand and a scone in the other, sipping and nibbling by turns, while her mind drifted from Cousin Arthur's arrival, to the coming meeting with Lord Lechton, to musing about their future. They had not discussed where they might live. Would Nate come home to the dower house in Oxfordshire with her and Elias?

She could not see him choosing to live with his father, whom he did not like above half, and Sarah was very much afraid that if she lived with Lady Lechton, she would soon find herself managing the entire household and Lady Lechton, too. Which would not be at all fair to the poor little mouse.

They would work something out. She and Nate. Something that suited their family.

19

Nate was also thinking about heroism. His need for Sarah had always been fierce, since their first tentative kiss all those years ago. The embers had flared when he set eyes on her again after seven years. The need to court her had driven the flames higher, and last night had done nothing to quench them.

If he'd thought about it, he would have expected his fear and anger during the chase to rescue her to be followed by intense craving. The need to affirm life was a common response to close brushes with death.

It was only right to keep a lid on the raging inferno of his yearning for her sweet body. She was hurt. She was tired and pale and determined to maintain her dignity.

But when she stripped before him, blushing so endearingly, it had been almost more than he could bear. Rather than turn into a ravishing brute, he had invented the errand to the nursery, though he'd realised as he spoke that Elias might well have heard something of the abduction, so it had been a necessary errand, as well as politic.

And he had better think about his son and the necessary explanations rather than his wife in her bath, or he would be in no fit case for the visit to come.

A boy's voice reached him as a footman let him into the children's realm on the third floor. Not his son's, but an older child's, with the occasional slip in vowels that identified him as Charlotte's rescued orphan, Tony.

"See, Master Elias? I told you Uncle Aldridge would rescue her."

"And my papa." That was Elias. "But Millie said he took Mama up to her chamber, and then sent down for medicine. She must be hurt, Tony."

"Now, then, Master Elias." An adult voice, female. The nurse? "If there is anything you need to know, you will be told. And that Millie will be feeling the rough edge of my tongue before she is very much older, you can be sure of that. Upsetting you with her stories."

"Can you not ask William to find out if my mother is hurt, Nanny?" Elias begged.

Nate entered the room and drew the eyes of the three occupants as he said, "A few bruises, Elias, and she is very tired after her adventure, but nothing more."

Elias leapt to his feet, pushing his chair over in his hurry to hurl himself at Nate. "Papa! Did you rescue her, Papa? Tony says his uncle did, but I told him his uncle has not been in the navy, as you have, Papa."

Nate caught him up and gave him a hug. Tony stayed seated, his splinted leg up on a stool before him, but bowed as well as he could. The nursemaid curtseyed. "You and Tony are both wrong," Nate explained. "Your mama rescued herself. She cut her bonds with a hidden knife, climbed out a window, and reached the roof of the building to which the kidnappers had taken her. She was on the roof by the time Lord Aldridge and I arrived, with the duke, your uncle Drew, and all of his men."

"Cor!" said Tony.

"Did you hit the bad men, Papa?" Elias wanted to know.

Nate sat for ten minutes, entertaining the boys with edited excerpts from the day's trials. He left them to their nurse when a footman brought in a tray with bread to toast and butter and jam to spread on it. "Go ahead and reprimand the maid Millie," he told the nursemaid before he left, "but also tell her that my lady may wish to speak to her about her loose tongue."

"She is not a bad girl, my lord," Morris assured him, "but she is foolish. I hope she will learn from this."

Nate met Drew on his way back to Sarah's chamber. "Is my cousin well?" the young lord asked.

"A few bruises and scrapes, and very tired. I left her at her bath while I went up to Elias. I'm now going to bind up the wound she sustained when she cut herself free from her bonds. Little more than a scratch, but it will do best not being rubbed on her bedding or sleeves. What news of the villains?"

"Locked up. The magistrate arrested the two women and the bawd pointed the finger at half a dozen of her men. Father has gone with Wakefield to Haverford House, where they expect to find Aldridge, who left not long after you did, and the person who warned him about the kidnapping. Tell Sarah we all send our love."

Nate agreed. He knocked on the door of the sitting room that Sarah shared with her sister, and let himself in when nobody answered, then knocked again at Sarah's bedchamber. This time, Lady Charlotte opened the door.

"Lord Bentham. Sarah is still in the bath."

"Come in, Nate," called his beloved, and Lady Charlotte stepped back out of the way, colouring almost as prettily as her sister did.

"Elias had heard something of the abduction," he told her, "and was arguing furiously with young Tony about whether you had been rescued by me or by his hero, his uncle Aldridge." He knelt by the tub to run a gentle finger over her cheek and smile into her eyes. "I told them you rescued yourself, and Aldridge and I arrived after the fact. They are both very impressed."

Sarah chuckled, and Nate leaned forward to touch her lips with his, in as gentle a salute as the brush of his finger. She clasped the back of his neck with a wet hand and pulled him in for a deeper kiss.

"I'll leave the two of you alone, then," Lady Charlotte said, surprising Nate, for he had forgotten she was in the room. He straightened and looked around, and frowned when he saw the maid was gone.

Sarah guessed his thoughts. "I sent Wilson away. I didn't need her with Charlotte here and you returning. Charlotte, darling, go and lie down again. Nate will look after me, now."

She held out her hand to her sister, who took it and bent over to peck Sarah's cheek. "Sleep well, Sarah. Good afternoon, Lord Bentham."

"Will you not call me Nate?" he asked, and she turned her smile on him.

"Nate, then. And you shall call me Charlotte. Good afternoon, Nate."

A large linen towel had been set ready on a chair next to the bathtub. Nate offered Sarah his hand to help her stand and step out of the water, and then wrapped the towel around her. His mouth had gone dry and his blood had rushed south, but he had no intention of imposing on his poor injured wife. "Come here by the fire, my love, and let me dry you," he said, and if he could hear the strain in his voice, he hoped she could not.

Drying her inch by delicious inch was a torture he did not want to end. The night rail left to warm before the fire was a sensuous concoction in silk that covered but outlined her shape. He helped her put on the matching robe, but it made little difference to the tempting package Sarah presented, warm from her bath, womanly shape almost visible through the concealing fabric, smelling of the herbs and flowers that perfumed her soap.

Her knife cut kept him tethered to her need for care, and he slathered it with the salve he had ready and wrapped it in a bandage, then kissed the poor bound wrist.

"Take me to bed, Nate," she murmured.

"Yes, of course," he answered, reminding himself again that she was almost an innocent and an injured one at that. "You must be tired."

"I am hungry," Sarah replied, a hint of irritation in her voice. "I am hungry for my husband's love, and tired of being treated as if I shall break at any moment. Take me to bed, Nate."

"Do you mean…?"

Sarah stamped one elegant bare foot. "Yes, I do."

"Thank God," Nate replied, and lifted her to carry her the few feet to the bed.

When Nate woke, a few last red streamers of cloud threaded the sky beyond the window. After sunset, then. Sarah slept snuggled into his arm, and he hated to move and risk waking her. Perhaps they should just stay here, and leave all that needed to be done until tomorrow.

She shifted her head, twisted and kissed his shoulder. "What time is it?" she murmured.

"After sunset. Perhaps between four thirty and five." On a deck at sea, clear of the smoke of London, he could be more precise. "Go back to sleep, my love."

But she pushed up to sitting. "I want to see Elias before I dress for dinner." She swung her feet over the side of the bed and, in the gloom, he could see her shadow between him and the embers of the fire. She turned around with a taper, which she lit to the two candles that stood in holders on the mantlepiece.

Nate sat up in the bed, the better to enjoy the sight of her walking naked across the room to collect her robe from the back of a chair.

She hesitated when she saw him watching. "Am I disturbing you, Nate?"

"Only in the best of all possible ways." No one served for long in the navy without becoming used to stripping off in front of other people. He pushed back the blankets and got out of bed, and had the satisfaction of seeing her eyes widen. With interest?

He hoped so, but she was right. They should see their son and then prepare for dinner, and if they were joining the family for dinner, he needed to go back to his rooms to change into suitable clothing. He said so.

"If you wish. But the clothes you wore to dinner last night have been cleaned and are hanging up in my dressing room. I'll just call for hot water, shall I?"

To save Wilson's sensibilities, Nate found and pulled on his pantaloons and his shirt from earlier in the day. "Yes, good. I will need to go back tomorrow, though. I can't expect your servants to keep one set of day wear and one of evening wear recycling day after day. I'll get Jackson to pack a bag for me."

Sarah had opened the door into the passage and given her message to the footman stationed there. She came back into the room looking pensive. "Do you think… It is over to you, Nate, but would it make sense for your manservant to pack all your things and bring them here? You could move in until we are ready to leave London.

"I know we have not discussed where we will live, and perhaps you would rather I came to stay with you, but I don't like to leave Elias, and I am assuming you do not wish to move in with your father. Though if you do, I would not object. Or if you think we should continue in our separate residences until our connection is public—"

He stopped her by placing a finger on her lips. "Moving in is an excellent idea, my love, if you have no objection, and if your uncle does not mind. I shall send a message to Jackson now, and tell him to give my notice to my landlady and present himself to me here tomorrow morning."

Sarah rewarded him with her glorious smile. "I shall tell Wilson to make space in my dressing room."

"Good, because Libby has insisted I need more clothes than I have ever had in my life. I have at least two dozen shirts, Sarah, would you believe? I have not had above a half dozen at a time since I was an infant in skirts!"

She kissed him at that, and then broke away to call Wilson into the room with hot water for their wash.

20

Sarah's cousin Ruth and her husband Val joined them for dinner, as did Arthur Beauclair and Uncle James's right-hand man, the guard commander Yousef. They kept the conversation light in front of the servants, but when they gathered in the drawing room afterwards, Sarah understood why Ruth and Val had been invited.

The warning about the abduction had come from Val's sister-in-law, sister to the felon known as the Beast, and herself wanted by the law for her part in an attack last year on Ruth and on Val's daughter. She had handed herself into the custody of Lord Aldridge, and was in the process of betraying her brother in return for a reward.

Val and Drew had joined Uncle James and Wakefield at Aldridge's house while Nate and Sarah caught up with their sleep.

"Elspeth wants immunity from prosecution and sufficient funds to travel to the Americas and set herself up there in some style," Val explained. "In return, she is willing to give us all the information she has about Stanley Wharton, including the plans he has set in motion."

Drew grimaced. "She says he has run mad. He is so obsessed with revenge on us and on Lord Aldridge that he cannot be reasoned with. He is throwing money at stupid plot after stupid plot, bribing and rewarding anyone who is prepared to attack us and any charity or business in the poorer parts of town that are associated with us. His sister says he is certain to bring himself down, and anyone allied with him."

"I do not like negotiating with vicious harridans who have injured me and my family," Uncle James commented, "but Wakefield points out that her information will help us mobilise the magistrates. At the moment, they are resisting the idea of invading the slums. Several of them are convinced that the multiple attacks are mere coincidence, and one informed me that ladies of consequence had no business in the kinds of charitable work that involved actually working with the poor."

"I think we should take Elspeth's offer," Ruth told them. "We want to get rid of her, do we not?"

"The female should not be rewarded for her evil," Yousef proclaimed.

Ruth shrugged. "Wherever she goes, she will make her own unhappiness, Yousef." She raised a hand and began counting off fingers. "I do not wish to see my husband's family name dragged through the gutters by the newssheets. Last year, when she escaped after her arrest, we managed to keep the story of her perfidy out of the printers' windows. If she goes to trial, she and our family will be pilloried in every ribald song and every caricature in every major city in the kingdom."

She put up the next finger. "Nor do I wish the gossipmongers of Society to grasp some of the salient details of her latest descent into the dregs of slums. What will it do to our daughters' reputations if people discover their aunt has been operating a brothel?"

She straightened a third. "Her information saved Sarah today. That is worth a great deal, whatever her motivations."

The fourth finger rose. "The information she promises us will cost as much or more to gain from other sources, and other people might be injured or even die as a result of the delay."

She straightened her thumb. "She, and Wharton, are simply not worth troubling ourselves over any more than it takes to stop them. I would like for us to be able to retire to the country for Christmas without concerns about returning to London to further such attacks."

Val was nodding, and so was Charlotte.

Drew complained, "She is a liar. How can we trust what she tells us?"

"Her demands are met only if her information proves true," Yousef suggested. "Her own life depends on her truth-telling." He shrugged and addressed Uncle James. "If you are willing, Yakub."

Uncle James frowned. "I dislike it, but it may be the best way to find and get rid of the vermin who are destroying all we are trying to do for those in need."

Sarah nodded to Ruth. "Our main goal must be to protect the schools and clinics and refuges, those who work in them, and those who turn to them for help. I agree with Ruth."

"What does Aldridge think?" Charlotte wondered, but apparently Aldridge had departed for Haverford Castle, leaving his mother in charge of his unwanted guest.

"The duchess will abide by our decision," Uncle James said.

Nate had a question of his own. "What of the Duke of Richport?"

"Gone," Uncle James replied. "His household here in London is closed up. His man of business says he left days ago for an extended world tour, but at the docks they told me that his ship sailed this afternoon."

"So, he escapes unpunished?" Nate growled.

The duke shrugged. "The bawd would not name him, and the men claim not to have met 'the gentleman' or to have been told who he is. He has gone, Nate. We will have to leave it at that. At least for the moment."

"The next point to discuss is how to present Nate's and Sarah's marriage to the Beau Monde," Ruth said.

"I plan to leave that to you ladies," Uncle James, "but I should tell you that the Duchess of Haverford is planning to visit tomorrow afternoon, once your mother and aunt arrive. She has some ideas on that matter."

"The duchess is an expert in the politics of the women's court," Ruth agreed. "She will be useful, Sarah. Father, we ladies shall manage the story of my cousin's marriage, and leave you gentlemen to get rid of the vermin."

The next day, two rooms in the Winshire townhouse took on the aspect of war rooms. The duke's study became the venue for the campaign to find and stop Wharton and his allies. Nate was included in the discussions, but soon discovered that only Arthur Beauclair had less experience in such planning than he, and even Cousin Arthur, with his experience at the Middlesex end of the Theodora Foundation, had more practical knowledge of slum life in London than did Nate.

Val Ashbury was a battle-hardened commander of men, and so were the duke and his sons, though they had learned in a different school, far away in Central Asia.

Nate made himself as useful as he could, conveying messages to and from other great houses, in between carrying out his duties at the temporary clinic that Ruth had established in a warehouse belonging to Lord Aldridge, and stealing moments with his wife and his son.

Sarah had commitments in the second of the war rooms: the ladies' drawing room. As predicted, Her Grace the Duchess of Haverford arrived shortly after Sarah's mother, the Dowager Lady Sutton, and her aunt, Lady Georgiana Winderfield.

Within the hour, Sarah came looking for Nate. "My mother and my aunts wish to meet you, Nate." He took her hand, feeling unaccountably nervous. Lady Sutton had every reason to despise the man who had run off with her daughter and then abandoned her, even if he had reasons, good reasons, for both actions.

He felt no better when he arrived in the drawing room, where three great ladies of Society sat side by side like justices in a courtroom, though they were seated on a long sofa behind a low table. Around them a number of other richly dressed ladies occupied chairs and couches. In his fancy, they would be the jury in the coming trial.

Sarah bobbed a curtsy. "Aunt Eleanor? Mama? Aunt Georgie? May I make known to you my husband, Lord Bentham?"

Nate bowed to each of them. He had seen the duchess at various entertainments this season; Lady Sutton, he recognised from years ago, when she'd attended church from Applemorn, which made the third Lady Georgiana, the duke's sister.

Sarah continued around the room. Charlotte, he knew, and Ruth. He also recognised the duchess's ward, Miss Grenford, with whom he had danced on the night he first waltzed with Sarah, who sat side by side with her sister, Lady Hamner.

The lady with the infant on her knee was the younger Lady Sutton. She was married to the duke's eldest son, who had arrived this afternoon with his wife and daughter, and immediately taken command of a large segment of the battle planning that continued in the study.

Nate was also presented to Lady Georgiana's friend, Miss Chalmers, and Lady Rosemary, another daughter of the duke.

Once he had been conducted around the room, he was instructed to sit. "There, Lord Bentham, if you please," said the dowager Lady Sutton. She pointed to a chair that had been placed a few feet away from and facing the long sofa. Again, he was uncomfortably reminded of a trial, an impression that was reinforced when Lady Sutton and Lady Georgiana nodded at the duchess, and she spoke.

"We are Sarah's godmother, mother, and aunt, Lord Bentham. We have stood beside her and suffered with her since you persuaded her to cast propriety to the wind and abscond with you and then disappeared."

She put up a hand when Nate opened his mouth, and he closed it again. She waited for a moment, as if to see whether he intended to continue his interruption, then nodded to Lady Sutton, who continued, "We understand that you were not responsible for your own abduction, but we wish to hear your explanation for the rest. Why did you elope with Sarah? Why did you not write to her? Why did you not return as soon as you were able?"

Lady Georgiana spoke next. "Sarah is satisfied. We understand that. But we saw what she went through, and Elias suffered too. If we are to promote the cause of your marriage to the *ton*, Lord Bentham, we must have some assurance that their happiness is important to you. And your past record is not reassuring."

Sarah put her hand on Nate's shoulder and protested, "Aunt Georgie!"

But Lady Sutton said, "We failed you seven years ago, Sarah, when we should have been your defence against your father and grandfather. We could not bear to fail you again."

Nate covered Sarah's hand with his own. "Ask your questions, my ladies, Your Grace. I will answer them to the best of my ability."

He had believed her uncle's cross-examination thorough. The ladies left the duke in their wake. They picked at every answer, taking him back over his actions and his motivations for his actions until he remembered things long forgotten.

He felt again the crushing fear that Sarah would be married off, all unwilling, to a care-for-nothing rakehell who would abuse and neglect her. Sutton had mentioned the Duke of Richport, famed in Applemorn for the orgies he held at his estate near there, and Viscount Rutledge, who was believed to have killed his first two wives and who certainly made them miserable.

At least those two men were relatively young, though both more than a decade older than Sarah. But Sarah's father also spoke of his own friends, and Sutton was a debauched old man—old, at least, in Nate's seventeen-year-old eyes—and one of Prinny's cronies, which made Nate think the man's friends would be even worse for Sarah than Richport or Rutledge.

Nate relived the exhilaration of realising the loophole formed by her technical residency of Sutton-Under-Swinwood. He recalled the nail-biting delays: waiting for Sarah to agree to come with him, waiting to see if anyone objected to the banns, waiting for Sarah to at last be his.

Most of his focus had to be on his three inquisitors, but Sarah's grip on his shoulder told him she shared the memories with him. Gasps and sighs from the younger ladies hinted that they, at least, favoured his case.

"Very well," Lady Sutton said, at last. "We agree that you acted in good faith, Lord Bentham, and with Sarah's well-being in mind. In hindsight, we might suggest you should have spoken to one of Sarah's female relatives about your concerns, but you were seventeen and a male. Now tell us what you remember of your abduction."

Not a great deal. He told them about being attacked on his way back from the village, about Elfingham's commands to the brutes who were beating him, and the jeered promise to Nate that Sarah would be wed to a proper gentleman, a peer, within the month. "That is the last thing I truly remember until I woke up far out to sea," he explained.

Which, of course, led to questions about what he half remembered—the random impressions of pain, jolting, voices, light and dark. Sarah's grip on his shoulder tightened to the point of pain.

They left that topic to ask about what happened once he was conscious again, and he told them about his desperate attempts to convince the doctor, and then the sailing master, that he had been abducted against his will, leaving behind a wife and a position as assistant secretary to the squire of Lesser Lechford. When, at last, he had been permitted to speak to a supercilious lieutenant who was technically in charge of the midshipmen, and who acted as gatekeeper to the captain, the man produced Nate's enlistment papers, signed by his father and witnessed by the Earl of Sutton.

The shadow of the despair that had possessed him for months after that revelation touched his soul once more. Only Sarah's hand, still gripping his shoulder, kept him anchored in the present. He swallowed hard and continued.

"I was not paid for nine months, and even then, since I was known to be aboard unwillingly, I was not permitted to disembark when we were in harbour. But I begged paper and ink and wrote letters—to Sarah, to my cousin Arthur, to my father, to a friend from the village that might have been able to send me news. The physician, Dr MacIntosh, agreed to post them for me. At every opportunity for a year after, I sent more. And I waited for replies."

A drop fell on the hand that rested over Sarah's and he looked around to see her crying. "I received none of your letters," she declared. He forgot the others in the room for a moment, needing only to comfort her, taking her hand and turning so he could look directly into her eyes. "I am here now, my love," he assured her, and she smiled through her tears and bent to kiss the corner of his lips.

"So, you gave up?" asked Lady Georgiana, recalling his attention to his inquisitors.

"I wrote less often," he replied. "After several years with no reply from anyone, yes, I gave up."

Lady Sutton echoed his own thoughts. "I truly do not see what else he could have done, Georgie, under the circumstances. But, Lord Bentham, were you never back in England?"

"No, my lady, nor anywhere in the United Kingdom until the navy sent me to Edinburgh two years ago to study medicine. I was there until my father decided a few months ago to question the navy about my supposed death. He had only the old duke's word for it, you see. He needed an heir, and arranged to have me discharged from the navy and returned to him."

He turned again to look at Sarah, this time standing and taking both of her hands in his. It was to her that he spoke his heart in front of them all. They had the right to hear because they loved her, but only she had the right to demand his reasons, his apologies, and his repentance.

"I convinced myself that you were married and out of my reach. I knew there would have been a scandal over the annulment that your father must have procured. I told myself it would be cruel to rake it all up again. But the truth is, I was afraid. Afraid to find you unhappily married and to have no right to do anything about it. Afraid to find you had married a man worthy of you, and forgotten all about the foolish mistake you made when you were still a girl."

He kissed her hands. "I have many regrets, my love, but that is the greatest. That I was too much of a coward to even ask about the Winshires for fear I would discover how you were, and that the truth, whatever it was, would break my heart all over again. We could have been together these last two years if I had just asked a few questions."

Sarah pulled her hands from his grasp and slid them around him, resting her head upon his breast when he used his to hold her closer. "You are here now," she reminded him.

"Which brings us to the present," said the Duchess of Haverford. "You met my goddaughter at a dinner here in London and discovered that she was not, in fact, married. How did you feel about that, Lord Bentham?"

Nate moved so he was facing the ladies again, looking at them over his wife's head. "That is not quite correct, Your Grace. My father suggested I come up to London to look for a wife. I had no interest in doing so. I already had a wife, whether that was legally true or not, and I had no intention of breaking the vows I made to her on our wedding day. But then…"

This memory was a pleasure after the harder ones that had booby-trapped the afternoon. Nate could feel the smile growing until a grin stretched his mouth. "Then he said that I need not consider Lady Sarah Winderfield, and I knew she had not married anyone else. I could not get to London quickly enough. When I arrived, I was told the Winshires were still out of town. I had no idea that my wife and her sister were in residence, or that they would be at dinner that night."

He placed a gentle kiss on Sarah's hair. "I saw her, more beautiful than ever, and I knew I had to try to win her back."

He was focused on Sarah, who had raised her mouth for his kiss heedless of their audience. He didn't see Lady Sutton rise and round the table that separated them; didn't know she was beside him till she tapped him on his shoulder and held out her arms for him.

"Allow me to give you a belated welcome to the family, my dear Nate. May I call you Nate? And may I apologise for what my husband and son did to you?"

He returned the hug wholeheartedly. "Yes, to the first, my lady. Mama, if I may be so bold. And no need to the second. I realise you were not consulted, and it is not your fault to apologise for."

The other ladies were lining up to give their own greetings. Lady Georgiana slapped him on the back and told him he was a good boy, and he should call her Aunt Georgie and her companion, who gave him her hand and a smile, Aunt Letty. The younger Lady Sutton said it would be less confusing for everyone if he just addressed her as Sophia. Miss Grenford declared that she was Jess to her friends. The most terrifying of them all, the Duchess of Haverford, wiped away a tear from the corner of her eye, insisting that he must call her Aunt Eleanor from this day on.

Someone must have notified the servants that the trial was over, for maids and footmen appeared with sumptuous refreshments, and the warm welcome to the family continued as two of the younger ladies poured and another two served everyone with their choice of tea, coffee or chocolate.

Nate found himself sitting on a little two-seater couch with Sarah at his side and a plate of sweet cakes and finely-cut sandwiches on a little table before them. The other ladies settled with their own choice of drink and edibles.

The Duchess of Haverford—Aunt Eleanor, and how the men he'd known in the navy would stare at him addressing a duchess in such an intimate fashion—called the meeting back to order.

"We have the essential elements of Nate's and Sarah's romance, ladies. Now we need to decide what to emphasise, and what to conceal."

Rosemary heaved a deep sigh. "It is such a romantic tale," she declared.

In a lesser lady, the smile the duchess gave might have been described as wicked. "Precisely," she said. "And that is how we shall present it."

"I propose," said Lady Sutton—Mama—"that we blame all the negative elements on Lord Sutton and the old duke, and credit Nate and Sarah with all the heroism."

"Of course," said Aunt Eleanor.

21

―――――

Curse all women to hell, and his sister to the deepest of the fiery pits. He should never have trusted the evil bitch. Never.

The Beast strode up and down the tiny room that he'd rented in a respectable boarding house in Southwark, too angry to sleep or even to sit still. Elspeth had double-crossed him. She had argued against his manifold stratagems to punish the two ducal families who had opposed him, and had then disappeared. The very next day he found his schemes collapsing around his ears as one ally after another was arrested.

Her betrayal was the only explanation, though he could not find out where she was. Just as well, perhaps, since his need to punish the ugly cow might have tempted him to risk his own escape for the pleasure of choking her to death with his own hands.

Instead, he had escaped before the Runners came to his own door, taking all the wealth he had in cash and portable objects, disguising himself in the salesman identity he had prepared for this very eventuality.

At least Elspeth knew nothing about Stephen Wheeler, manufacturer of fine buttons, nor about the plump and juicy bank accounts and investments the Beast had in that name. He even had a house in the Midlands, where Wheeler would be welcomed when he returned from a prolonged overseas trip.

Which would be within the next few weeks. Only one thing still kept him in London, trusting in his disguise to keep him from arrest. He waited for word that the men he had hired had carried out the Beast's final commission.

His last piece of unfinished business was the boy Tony. He had people watching the house to try another kidnapping as soon as the boy left it, but if that was out of the question, the sharpshooter he had hired would ensure that, if the Beast could not have Tony, neither would that prissy arrogant ass Aldridge.

22

———

Both campaigns proceeded smoothly.

"The Beast has disappeared," Wakefield reported. "We can find no trace of his movements."

"Annoying," commented the duke. Uncle James. Nate was still coming to terms with addressing him so intimately.

"Dealing with others in the plots he set up is easier without him," Jamie, the duke's eldest son, pointed out. "Many of his allies are turning on him."

"Yes," Wakefield agreed. "And their information is making it easy to mop up those who don't."

As to Nate's and Sarah's marriage, it was a romance to be celebrated and not a scandal to be decried, just as Rosemary had said. "Mama, Aunt Eleanor, and Aunt Georgie decree it to be so," Sarah told Nate. "Their equally powerful friends concur. Therefore, everyone who wants to be accepted in Society is in agreement."

Only close friends and immediate family were able to speak to the couple in question. Nate and Sarah were under firm instructions to be seen from a distance. They rode by in a carriage too quickly to do more than nod at any greeting. They visited the duck pond in Green Park with their son and Nate's sisters surrounded by Winshire's fierce servants, who politely requested any who dared approach to respect the family's privacy and move along. They appeared in the Winshire box at the Opera with Lord and Lady Lechton, arriving after the curtain rose and leaving before it fell, and thus avoiding any contact with the curious or intrusive.

Visitors who arrived at either the Winshires or the Lechtons were informed that the little family was taking the time to enjoy their reunion, and were not accepting callers.

"Everywhere we go," Jamie's wife Sophia said, "we are besieged with questions."

Charlotte laughed. "We tell everyone how delighted we are that the Benthams have found one another again and been reunited with their son."

Ruth's eyes twinkled. "And if they wish to know more, Nate, we refer them to your father."

Nate grinned. Lord Lechton, clearly besotted with his grandson, described in detail to anyone who would listen to him the boy's amazing accomplishments and Lady Bentham's many virtues.

"He would be less delighted," Nate whispered to Sarah, "if your female relatives had not absolved him of any responsibility for our separation."

Sarah was more sympathetic. "You did not know my grandfather," she argued. "Your father was bullied into signing those papers, Nate, as you well know. Quite right for all the blame to placed where it belongs. On my father and grandfather."

The only flaw in Lechton's happiness was that 'the fruit of his loins' had refused to obey the paternal command to bring his wife and son to live in Lechton's household. "We are going to Winds' Gate for Christmas with Sarah's family," Nate told him. "We will visit you in the new year, Father. We have signed a lease on a town-house here in London, to start in March. We will come up to town for at least part of the Season."

Sarah, always kinder to Lechton than Nate felt able to be, added, "You will be pleased to know, sir, that we are seeking a country house in Oxfordshire, midway between Swinwood where my mother lives and Three Oaks at Lechford. We will not be more than a couple of hours away, so you will be able to see Elias often."

With that, Lord Lechton had to be content.

By the evening of the famed end-of-season ball, the Polite World's excitement over finally meeting Lord and Lady Bentham was at a peak. Nate teased Sarah, "My head aches at the mere thought of all the gawking and gossiping ton. I might take a tisane and go to bed instead of dressing for the evening." He was only half joking.

His man Jackson treated the comment with the contempt he felt it deserved, only recommending, "Keep still, my lord," as he shaved his master in front of one of a pair of mirrors, while Wilson dressed Sarah's hair in front of the other. The couple had fallen into the habit of partially dressing one another, then donning robes to avoid laccrating the sensibilities of their servants. And of Nate, come to think of it. He had no wish for Jackson to be present in the room when Sarah was unclothed.

Sarah laughed at Nate's teasing. "It will soon be over, dearest. That is lovely, Wilson."

Nate, at a point in his shave where turning his head might have unfortunate consequences, tried to catch a glimpse of his wife, but she had whisked herself away to the bed with Wilson in attendance, and he had to wait for Jackson to pat him dry before he could turn and see her.

Lovely in a green gown embroidered heavily in gold and silver, and trimmed with delicate falls of lace, she stood patiently waiting for Wilson to finish fastening her laces and her buttons. Her hair was dressed high; curls studded with diamond-headed pins, finished with a fantasy of a tiara in gold with pearls, diamonds and emeralds. The tiara was part of a set: a dainty necklace circled her throat and earrings dropped from her lobes. The matching bracelet sat on the dressing table, waiting for Sarah to don her gloves.

"Stunning," Nate told her. Beyond stunning, if there were such a thing. Every time he saw her, he felt it as a benign blow to the head that managed to send him dizzy without causing pain.

"I have remembered another great advantage of marriage,"

Sarah crowed. "I am now permitted to wear a tiara! Isn't the set delightful?"

"Delightful," he agreed, though he meant her rather than the jewellery her uncle had given her the day before.

He allowed Jackson to tie his cravat and to hand him the waistcoat he was to wear—green like his lady's gown and embroidered to match. The coat came next, and his gloves. By the time he was finished, so was Sarah, and she tugged him in front of the mirror so that they could admire one another and the picture they made together.

She was bubbling with excitement, and if Nate did not feel quite so pleased with the idea of the coming evening, that was of no account. Sarah was happy and therefore so was he.

It had been a wonderful evening. Sarah thought so, and all the ladies agreed when they gathered with their husbands and children at Fournier's pastry shop early the following afternoon. They were all leaving town the next day, and the children had been keen for one more meeting before they went their separate ways.

Pouring rain put the park out of the question, the children declared their own nurseries boring, and everyone decided that another foray to the purveyor of wonderful little cakes would be delightful.

Once again, the children had their own table. This time, Tony had been included, carried out to the carriage and into the tea rooms by a pair of footmen. Elias sat on one side of him with Lechton's two older daughters beside him, and on the other side of Tony were the two Ashbury girls.

The nursemaids sat close by, with the littlest Lechton daughter and the Sutton's pride and joy, each sitting on their own nurse's knee, babbling and waving energetically at the other.

Sarah's eyes kept sliding to the two sweet baby girls. She would like one just like that. Elias was precious and much loved, but she had missed his entire infancy. Beside her, Ruth was watching the babies, too, her hand unconsciously cupped across the abdomen where her own baby thrived and grew towards its birth.

Sarah found her own hand creeping to her stomach. Perhaps, even now…

While the women rehashed the ball, and shared the various attempts of the worst of the gossips to find some scandal broth to spice up their evening, the men were commiserating with one another about the fight in the slums being over, or at least that was how it sounded to Sarah.

Not her father-in-law. He was making a last-ditch attempt to persuade Nate to change his mind about spending Christmas at Winds' Gate, until Uncle James intervened. "The Benthams will come to us this Christmas, Lord Lechton, as we have planned." He added, kindly, "You and your wife and daughters are very welcome to join us at Wind's Gate next year for Christmas. I shall not expect you to change your plans this year."

A wail brought the adults' attention to the children. The middle Lechton child, Lavie, was standing on her chair weeping as if her heart would break, an orange stain running down her pinafore from a ball of flavoured ice that decorated her chest, a splosh of orange liquid on her cheek showing the point of impact.

Since Elias was the only child to have an orange-coloured ice, the culprit was obvious.

All of the other children turned wary eyes on their parents, and Elias turned white. "I am sorry, Mama," he said, as Libby hurried to soothe her daughter and the nursemaid efficiently mopped away the worst of the mess.

Sarah and Nate moved to flank their son, and Elias seemed to shrink in his chair, looking up at his father. He didn't hesitate, though he gulped before he spoke. "I did not mean to do it, Papa. I was showing Tony how I could make the ball of ice jump, and it jumped too far."

"Then you owe Lady Lavinia an apology, Elias," Nate told him gravely.

"We do not play with our food, Elias," Sarah added. "To help you remember that fact, on our next visit to Gunthers or Fournier's with your aunts, you will not be permitted to have an ice."

Tony was hunching as if he thought, if he tried hard enough, his head might retract like a turtle's into its shell. "It was my fault, my lady. I wagered he could not flick the ball up off the spoon and catch it again." He swallowed. "I deserve to be punished, too."

By the time Charlotte had been summoned to pronounce judgement on her protégé, and both boys had apologised to a tear-stained but composed Lavie, the babies were raising their voices in a wail that proclaimed tea time was over. The whole party packed up, shrugged into coats, raised umbrellas and began to decamp from the front door.

The unmarked anonymous carriage that raced to a halt in front of them seemed to come out of nowhere. Before most of them could push their way from the shop, the carriage door flew open and a man put down one foot and reached out to grab Elias, who had been one of the first to leave, hand-in-hand with Lavie.

From inside the window, Sarah could see it all—Elias being dragged towards the carriage, Lechton throwing himself on the would-be kidnapper's arm, two of Uncle James's guard suddenly surging into action from the other side of the carriage, one knocking the driver to the ground and taking the reins, and the other dropping from the roof onto the shoulders of the man hanging out of the door.

The family spilt out onto the footpath, clustering around, all talking at once. Sarah had almost reached her son when Lechton gave an exclamation and threw himself on top of the boy. As two red stains bloomed on the back of her father-in-law's jacket, Sarah realised that the sound she had heard was gunfire.

Cousin Jamie pointed up to the roof of the building across the street. "There!" he shouted, and raced off with several of the other men beside him. Nate was kneeling next to his father, as Ruth helped Elias out from underneath him. "Your son is unhurt," she assured Sarah, giving Elias into her arms. She sank down beside Nate.

"Is Grandpapa dead?" Elias wanted to know. Sarah met Libby's eyes, and they were asking the same question over the top of Lavie and Norie, who were burrowed into her arms.

"Papa and Auntie Ruth are helping him," Sarah consoled them all.

They moved Lord Lechton carefully back into Fournier's out of the rain. Val raced off to the Ashton carriage and came back with Ruth's medical kit. Nate and Ruth sent the other adults off to a far corner to look after the children and wait.

At one point, Nate caught Sarah's eye and shook his head. At another, Jamie and Drew returned to report they had caught the sharpshooter. "He and the kidnappers were paid by the Beast," Jamie said.

"But why?" Sarah had finally released Elias, who was sitting with his arms around two of his little aunts. Drew beckoned Sarah and Charlotte to follow him a few paces away from the children and whispered, "They were after Tony. He told them if they couldn't get the boy to kill him. I'm sorry, Sarah. They didn't know there were two boys."

It was all just a tragic mistake, though Sarah couldn't help but be glad that both boys had survived. "You will have to make sure Tony is somewhere Wharton will never find him," she said to Charlotte.

After a long time, Nate approached Libby. "I am so sorry, Libby," he said. "We could not stop the bleeding."

Libby burst into tears, and Sarah felt like crying, too, at the look on her husband's face. "Shall we take the children home?" she asked.

"Good idea. I will have to stay to talk to the coroner. I will be home as soon as I can, my love."

"I will be at your father's house, with Libby," Sarah told him.

In the end, they did not leave London for another two days, and then made haste to Lechford for Lord Lechton's funeral, all of the Winshire family coming along in support.

The reading of the will had Libby in tears. Lechton had left her a substantial annuity to supplement the dower stipulated in her marriage settlements, and accompanied them with an exhortation to be open to marrying again. "For she has been a good wife, and she and our daughters have brought much joy to this old man's heart. I would wish her to find the happiness she richly deserves."

Even so, he left the guardianship of said daughters to Nate, whom he called, "My beloved son, who is safely back in his family's embrace after all his travels." Nate was also appointed trustee, along with Cousin Arthur—"one of the most honest men I know"—of the dowries set aside for the three girls.

Apart from some minor legacies to servants, everything else went to Nate, either as the new earl, or as a personal bequest.

That evening, Nate wandered off after dinner, saying that he would be back soon. It was a fine evening, and the half moon gave plenty of light, so after an hour Sarah set off in search of him. As she expected, she found him in the little graveyard next to the Lechton family tomb, gazing sombrely on the ornate gothic carving.

"I did not want to be earl," he told Sarah, as she sat down beside him and took his hand. "Not ever, and certainly not so soon."

"I know," she answered.

"I wanted enough time to… I don't know. Learn to stop being angry with him, I suppose. I think I have resented him all my life, Sarah. It wasn't just what happened to us. Even before that… When my mother was alive, she would always tell me how important he was, how wise, how worthy. I barely saw him, but that was because he was busy doing God's work. Then she died, and I grew older, and found that he was an insignificant man in an isolated parish, foolish and too much concerned with appearances and status. I was required to obey him, but he was not someone I could respect." Tears were running down his cheeks.

Sarah couldn't think of anything to say. She had hated her own father and had come to hate her brother, but Lord Lechton had not been the kind of monster Sutton was. Just, as Nate said, a foolish man obsessed with status. She squeezed Nate's hand, hoping it would be some kind of comfort.

"His will! Libby told me she had no idea that he thought her a good wife. Isn't that sad?"

Sarah could only nod. Libby had said the same thing to her, accompanied by gushes of tears.

"He was a good landlord; did you know that? Several of his tenants today told me of kindnesses. A child's school fees paid. A rebate on rent in hard times. Perhaps, if I had not been so angry, so distant, when he sent for me, I would have learned these things, Sarah."

"You are learning now," Sarah said. "And you are learning to stop being angry with him. He was only a man, Nate. If my father and grandfather had not bullied him, he would not have betrayed us. He was not a bad man." Damning with faint praise, that. She tried again. "He was a good man, in a way."

"Perhaps. Probably. Yes, you are right." His sudden laugh surprised Sarah. "I suppose it would pay for me to stop expecting perfection from my own father now that I have a son who will one day stand in judgement on me from the lofty eminence of his first quarter century."

He kissed her ear. "Thank you for coming to find me. Is everyone ready for the grand procession tomorrow?"

They were leaving for Wind's Gate, taking Libby and the girls along with them. And they would return here after Christmas. Nate's mind must have tracked with Sarah's, for he laughed again and said, "My father got his own way after all. You and I will be living here at Three Oaks. Come on, darling. Let us go inside. Let us go to bed."

They walked back along the path from the church to the house, hand in hand. Just outside the side door that she had left unlatched for their return, he stopped to kiss her again. "I could not face all of this without you, my dearest heart."

She looked up into his beloved face, turned to planes and shadows in the moonlight, his eyes smiling into hers. "You and I have both shown that we have the strength to stand alone if we must," she said. "How much better to be able to show the world how strong we are together."

The new Earl of Lechton bent to lift his countess, and carried her upstairs to bed.

<h1 style="text-align:center">EPILOGUE</h1>

March 1815

In the early Spring, Charlotte came up to London to support Sarah and her husband. Charlotte and Sarah sat in the public gallery of the House of Lords, watching as the Earl of Lechton, resplendent in his parliamentary robes and flanked by two other earls, made his formal presentation of his credentials to the clerk. The following day, Charlotte and Nate waited in one of the outer rooms of St James Palace while the twin's mother presented the Countess of Lechton at a drawing room presided over by the Prince Regent.

A ball hosted by Lord and Lady Lechton at the Winshire mansion, the Lechton townhouse being too small, rounded out the events that marked Nate's and Sarah's full ascension to the honours and duties of their new position.

"They seem devoted to one another still," Aldridge commented, as he and Charlotte took their turn to stand out of the line in the set they were dancing.

"They are," Charlotte assured him. "I have never seen Sarah so happy. When she found Elias, she said that she had all she needed in life, but there was always an edge of sadness—and now it is gone. She and Nate complete one another, I think."

Charlotte didn't mean to sigh. She hoped Aldridge wouldn't think her jealous of Sarah's happiness. His comment showed he understood, as he turned his head to watch his half-sister Lady Hamner skip down through the pattern of the dance, her eyes fixed on her husband. "I see Matilda and Charles, so absorbed in one another the rest of us might as well not exist. And I am pleased for them, of course. It makes me wistful, Cherry."

Wistful described her feelings perfectly. She was so pleased with his understanding that she accepted his request for another dance, this one a waltz, and then regretted it when he put his hand on her back, just above the waist, and the uncomfortable sensations that only he inspired possessed her.

"They dance beautifully together," Nate observed to his wife as they watched Charlotte and Aldridge in the waltz. "It is obvious they care for one another."

Sarah shook her head. "I wish… But I understand her reasons for refusing him, Nate."

"She should tell him her reasons," Nate argued. "Does he not have a right to know why he is being rejected?

"She will not, though. She is afraid he would insist it doesn't matter, then come to hate her. And she could never bear that. I wish he were not heir to a duke, Nate. She might take the risk with an ordinary gentleman."

"I imagine he will be the Duke of Haverford before the end of this year," Nate observed. "I wonder if that is what Colyton is waiting for?"

The Earl of Colyton was dancing with Jessica. According to the Duchess of Haverford, he had been very attentive since the duchess and her two younger wards had arrived back in Town earlier in the month.

His caution in coming to the point was understandable, Sarah supposed, given that his chosen wife would also be stepmother to his daughters. Sarah could not forget his scathing denouncement of base-born children in high-born families, but perhaps he had changed his mind.

"Here comes Val," Sarah said. The Earl of Ashbury had attended the House of Lords investment, the luncheon after the Drawing Room, and now the ball at the behest of his wife, who had not come to London with him.

"A good turn out," he said to the couple. "Sarah, what do you call that colour you are wearing? Ruth will want to know."

"Lavender stripes on an ivory base with Esterhazy lace," Sarah told him.

Val grinned. "I can manage to remember lavender and ivory. I thought you were going to say 'maiden's sigh', or 'Princess Royal' or some obscure French word invented by dress-makers to confuse the rest of us. Mirrie asked me to fetch her Coquelicot ribbons and Genny wanted hers in Pompadour, if you can believe it."

"When are you heading home?" Sarah asked.

"Tomorrow, as I had planned."

Nate widened his eyes. "I thought the news from France might…" he trailed off at a nudge from his wife.

Val responded to the comment anyway. "I cannot make much of a contribution to stopping Napoleon. I can be with my wife when our child is born." He shrugged. "There's a lot of posturing in the House of Lords, but this is not going to have a political solution. We will need to fight the man again." He shrugged the shoulder above his empty sleeve. "I can't make a contribution there, either, and better tacticians than I are buzzing in and out of the Foreign Office and the Horse Guard."

"Give your ladies my love," Sarah said. "Do you think you'll bring them up to town before the end of the Season?"

Val shook his head. "Not with Wharton still at large somewhere. It's too hard to protect them in London."

"That's what we decided about my sisters and Elias," Nate told him.

"Wakefield and his agents are following every possible lead,"

Sarah pointed out. "And we have had no trouble since my kidnapping. Perhaps he is dead, or has left the country."

Nate and Val didn't comment, but she knew what they were thinking. Until they had proof positive the evil man would trouble them no more, they would continue to worry about their families.

The waltz drew to a close, and Aldridge escorted Charlotte towards them. The men began a vigorous discussion about the reaction of the French army to the triumphal progress through France of their deposed Emperor, and Sarah drew Charlotte to one side. "Your waltz was a beautiful thing to see, dearest."

Charlotte grimaced. "I know what you're thinking. It can never happen, Sarah." She nodded to where Uncle James was talking to Aunt Eleanor. "That might, when she is widowed."

Sarah was diverted. "I believe you are right, and I wish them joy."

"So do I," Charlotte replied. "They have waited a long time."

As they watched, the duke and the duchess inclined their heads and parted. Their demeanour, at least in public, was above reproach, but his eyes followed her as she walked away.

Sarah said, "I am going to go and sit down for a while, Charlotte. Come and keep me company?"

Nate overheard. "Are you well, dearest? Do you need to go home?"

"And you a doctor!" she scolded. "I am perfectly well, if a little tired. And I am certainly not leaving the ball at which I am hostess!"

"I will make her sit down and have a bite to eat, Nate," Charlotte told him. "You look after your guests." She grinned at him. "This is all your fault, you know."

"Fruit of your loins," Sarah teased.

The two women strolled through into the supper room and Nate flushed as he turned back to his cousin-in-law and his would-be brother-in-law, hoping they had not heard.

"I take it," Val commented, "that congratulations are in order." *So much for that.*

"Yes," said Aldridge. "Every best wish to you and your growing family, Lechton. May your happiness always increase."

How can I be happier? Nate wondered, as he accepted their congratulations. Still, the last few months suggested his capacity for happiness could grow. When Sarah accepted him back into her life and Elias's, he had thought his happiness complete. And then Elias had called him Papa. And then he became accustomed to the pleasure of waking up beside his wife. And then she told him she was with child again.

Yes, his happiness increased as his love for Sarah grew—another thing he would not have thought possible three months ago. "If you'll excuse me, gentlemen, I am under instructions to look after our guests," he told Val and Aldridge. "I should circulate, and make sure everyone is having a good time."

But first, he followed the sisters to the supper room, not to interrupt their conversation—they were enjoying a comfortable coze at one of the tables—but simply to let his eyes rest for a moment on the woman he loved, his safe harbour and his heart's companion. The long journey was over and a new and better one was well begun.

THE END

But wait. There's more.

For Charlotte's and Aldridge's story, look for *To Tame the Wild Rake*, now on preorder. The love story of the Duke of Winshire and the Duchess of Haverford will conclude in *Paradise At Last*, to be published before the end of 2021 as part of *The Paradise Triptych* (*Paradise Regained*, *Paradise Lost*, and *Paradise at Last*).

Find more information and buy links at https:// judeknightauthor.com/books/

Do you like news before anyone else, plus discounts, and free stuff?

Sign up to my newsletter. The main newsletter goes out once every two months, and includes news about coming books, discounts, contests, and events. Every newsletter also has news about books from my author friends, and a free story that I write just for newsletter subscribers.

In between newsletters, if I have something exciting to share I occasionally sends a one-topic email.

Free book as a thank you

As a thank you for subscribing to my newsletter, you can expect a series of three emails, the first offering a free copy of one of my books, and the next two with links to other free stories. So why not subscribe today?

Subscribe to newsletter: http://judeknightauthor.com/newsletter/

ENJOY THESE BOOKS BY JUDE KNIGHT

Regency books

The Return of the Mountain King series

James Winderfield, exiled third son of the Duke of Winshire, is back to inherit the ducal title.

In 1812, high Society is rocked by the return of the Earl of Sutton, heir to the dying Duke of Winshire. James Winderfield, Earl of Sutton, Winshire's third and only surviving son, has long been thought dead, but his reappearance is not nearly such a shock as those he brings with him, the children of his deceased Persian-born wife and fierce armed retainers, both men and women.

The Duke of Haverford, his one-time rival in love, sets out to destroy him, and his children with him, but Sutton is no longer the friendless, open-hearted youth that was exiled for his temerity. Even inheriting his father's title won't stop his enemies from trying to kill him. But no one, his people whisper, ever wins against the King of the Mountains.

As the new Duke of Winshire's four older children and his twin nieces navigate society to find acceptance and a love of their own, Winshire rekindles his acquaintance with the influential and beloved matriarch, Eleanor, Duchess of Haverford. Their time is long past; their friendship, though, is golden.

Paradise Regained (prequel novella)

James yearns to end a long journey in the arms of his loving family. But his father's agents offer the exiled prodigal forgiveness and a place in Society — if he abandons his foreign-born wife and children to return to England.

With her husband away, Mahzad faces revolt, invasion and betrayal in the mountain kingdom they built together. A queen without her king, she will not allow their dream and their family to be destroyed.

To Wed a Proper Lady — The Barbarian and the Bluestocking (novel 1 in the series)

Everyone knows James needs a bride with impeccable blood lines. He needs Sophia's love more.

James, eldest son of the Earl of Sutton, must marry to please his grandfather, the Duke of Winshire, and to win social acceptance for himself and his father's other foreign-born children. But only Lady Sophia Belvoir makes his heart sing, and to win her, he must invite himself to spend Christmas at the home of his father's greatest enemy: the man who is fighting in Parliament to have his father's marriage declared invalid and the Winderfield children made bastards.

Sophia keeps secret her *tendre* for James, Lord Elfingham. After all, the whole of Society knows he is pursuing the younger Belvoir sister, not the older one left on the shelf after two failed betrothals. Even when he asks for her hand in marriage, she still can't quite believe that he loves her.

(This book was first published as a novella, and has been extensively rewritten to make it a novel. The novella was in the Bluestocking Belles' collection *Holly and Hopeful Hearts*.)

A Suitable Husband

A chef from the slums, however talented, is no fit mate for the cousin of a duke, however distant. But Cedrica Grenford can dream. (novella)

To Mend the Broken-Hearted — The Healer and the Hermit (Novel 2)

Trained as a healer, Ruth Winderfield is happiest in a sickroom. When she's caught up in a smallpox epidemic and finds herself quarantined at the remote manor of a reclusive lord, the last thing she expects is to find her heart's desire. A pity he does not feel the same. She must return to London's ballrooms, where the wealth of her family and the question over her birth make her a target for the unscrupulous and a pariah to the high-sticklers.

Valentine, Earl of Ashbury, is horrified when an impertinent bossy female turns up with several sick children, including the two girls he is responsible for. He hasn't seen his niece and his daughter—if she is his daughter—since his faithless wife and treacherous brother died three years ago. He reluctantly gives them shelter. Even more reluctantly, he helps with the nursing.

When Ruth goes, she takes his heart with him. When jealous relatives lie about their time together, Val must face his past and win her back, not just for himself, but for the children he has come to love.

Melting Matilda (A novella in the Bluestocking Belle's collection, Fire & Frost, published as stand-alone in May 2021)

Sparks flew a year ago when the Granite Earl kissed the Ice Princess under the mistletoe. Matilda Grenford is a lady and the ward of a duchess, but the daughter of a famous courtesan. Charles, Earl of Hamner, seeks a countess of impeccable bloodlines, not one whose scandalous birth would offend every noble ancestor back to the Norman Conquest. But neither of them can forget that kiss.

To Claim the Long-Lost Lover — The Diamond and the Doctor (this book)

Sarah Winderfield has refused dozens of marriage offers since Nathaniel Beauclair convinced her to run away with him eight years ago, and then disappeared without a word or a trace. But now she needs a husband. She has a child to love and to protect, and the child needs a father.

She does not expect to meet Nate when she ventures back into the marriage mart. Should she let him explain why he deserted her? Can she believe him?

Dragged back to England to feed his father's pride in family, Nate refuses to give into the man's demands that he take a wife. But his father mentions Sarah Winderfield, he rushes to London. Those who beat and abducted him insisted that she was to be married within the month, but she is still single. Surely they can find again the promise they believed in when they were young?

Through a labyrinth of old rumours and new enemies, two long-lost lovers must decide whether or not to claim one another, and win the bright future they both desire.

Coming in September 2021

To Tame the Wild Rake — The Sinner and the Saint

The Marquis of Aldridge doesn't want to yearn for the sister of a friend from his raking days. Especially since she has rejected him in no uncertain terms. Charlotte Winderfield, niece of the Mountain King, keeps a secret that bars her from marriage, but even if she found the courage to trust, she would never trust a rake.

The Golden Redepennings series

True love is rare and elusive, but they won't settle for less.

Candle's Christmas Chair (A novella in *The Golden Redepennings* series)

They are separated by social standing and malicious lies. He has until Christmas to convince her to give their love another chance.

<u>*Gingerbread Bride*</u> (A novella in *The Golden Redepennings* series)

Mary runs from an unwanted marriage and finds adventure, danger and her girlhood hero, coming once more to her rescue.

Farewell to Kindness (Book 1 in *The Golden Redepennings* series)

Love is not always convenient. Anne and Rede have different goals, but when their enemies join forces, so must they.

A Raging Madness (Book 2 in *The Golden Redepennings* series)

Their marriage is a fiction. Their enemies are all too real. Uncovering the truth will need all the trust Ella and Alex can find.

The Realm of Silence (Book 3 in *The Golden Redepennings* series)

Rescue her daughter, destroy her dragons, defeat his demons, return to his lonely life. How hard can it be?

Unkept Promises (Book 4 in *The Golden Redepennings* series)

Mia hopes to negotiate a comfortable marriage. Jules wants his wife to return to England, where she belongs. Love confounds them both.

Other Regency books

A Baron for Becky

She was a fallen woman. How could the men who loved her help set her back on her feet?

House of Thorns

His rose thief bride comes with a scandal that threatens to tear them apart.

Lord Calne's Christmas Ruby

One wealthy merchant's heiress with an aversion to fortune hunters. One an impoverished earl with a twisted hand. Combine and stir with one villainous rector. (novella)

Revealed in Mist

As spy and enquiry agent, Prue and David worked to uncover secrets, while hiding a few of their own.

The Beast Next Door (A novella in the Bluestocking Belles collection *Valentines from Bath)*

In all the assemblies and parties, no-one Charis met could ever match the beast next door.

Lunch-length reads: story collections

Hand-Turned Tales and Lost in the Tale

A double handful of short stories and novellas. *Hand-Turned Tales* is free from most eretailers. Try the range of Jude's imagination one bite at a time, in a lunch-length read.

If Mistletoe Could Tell Tales

A repackaging of six published Christmas stories: four novellas and two novelettes. Because nothing enhances the magic of Christmas like the magic of love.

Hearts in the Land of Ferns

Five stories all set in New Zealand: two historical and three contemporary suspense. All That Glisters has been published in Hand-Turned Tales. The other four have all been published in multi-author collections, but never before in a collection of Jude Knight stories.

ABOUT JUDE KNIGHT

I've always wanted to be a novelist. I was a good enough reader to see that the first two attempts (one when I was fourteen and one in my early twenties) weren't good enough to publish. Then along came life. A seriously ill child who required years of therapy; a rising mortgage that led to a full-time job; my own chronic illness… the writing took a back seat.

As the years passed, the fear grew. I'd waited so long. If I never finished any of the dozens of novels I started, no one would ever judge them.

My mother believed in me, and on the way home from that great lady's funeral, I realised I'd left it too late for Mum to ever hold a print copy of one of my fiction books. So I replaced the fear of finishing with the fear of not finishing, by telling everyone I knew that I was writing a novel.

In the years since I published my first fiction book just before Christmas in 2014, I've published eleven novels, as many novellas, a heap of shorter stories, and more novellas in group anthologies. I plan to keep going till I run out of years.

I write historical fiction with a large helping of romance, a splash of Regency, and a twist of suspense.

I then try to figure out how to slot it into a genre category.

I'm mad keen on history, enjoy what happens to people in the crucible of a passionate relationship, and love to use a good mystery and some real danger as mechanisms to torture my characters.

In my other identity as Judy Knighton, I've been a plain language consultant specialising in contracts, insurance policies, and financial disclosure statements. Fiction is more fun.

Website and blog: http://judeknightauthor.com/
Book blurbs and links: http://judeknightauthor.com/books/

www.ingramcontent.com/pod-product-compliance
Lightning Source LLC
Chambersburg PA
CBHW021657110726
47902CB00007B/1968